TWO WEEKS TO LOVE

Decker Springs Book 1

JENNIFER HOOPES

Jennifer Hoopes

P.O. Box 563

Manchester, PA 17345

Two Weeks to Love (Decker Springs, Book 1)

Edited by Laura Barth

Cover design by LLewellen Designs

First edition published 2019

Printed in the United States of America

Print edition ISBN: 978-1-7337523-1-2

Digital edition ISBN: 978-1-7337523-0-5

Chapter 1

Kat Evans blew a strand of hair out of her face and groaned. This story had more plot holes than Swiss cheese and, to be perfectly frank…sucked. Big time. Like, lollipop sucked.

She knew it. Her agent knew it. And based on the number of comment bubbles currently mocking her from her laptop, her editor knew it too.

The problem was she had a deadline, didn't know how to fix half the issues, and refused to ask for an extension. Women set on hoeing their own row did not ask for extensions. Sighing, she closed her eyes and tried some rhythmic breathing. If she was being honest, the root of all her plot problems was her personal life, or rather the remnants of her personal life. Shame she couldn't escape the train wreck of this story the way she'd escaped her groom.

"Umm, excuse me, this is my table."

What was keeping her hero and heroine apart? How could she beef up what was currently a conflict with as much weight as a feather? Of course there would be a happily-ever-after, but how could she torture them before they got there?

"My table. This is it."

Opening her eyes, she dropped her chin onto her hand. The words on the screen resembled a Rorschach of failure. Maybe she could add a dog? Readers loved dogs. Maybe if she added enough of them, readers wouldn't realize there was no story to follow. Dogs deserved happily-ever-afters, right?

"That should be 'too' with two *o*'s not one *o*, and you're missing quite a few commas. There, there…"

A finger came from the left field to jab at her screen, and Kat whirled around, a loud shriek bouncing off the brick of a man beside her.

"Who knew grammar was the way to get your attention?"

The brick straightened, and Kat bet her eyes matched the size of the saucer her teacup currently sat on. He was tall. No, she was a writer, dammit, tall was too mild. He loomed in her space, sucking up all the oxygen and leaving dizziness in its wake. Not to mention a healthy dose of insta-lust.

His head—which was covered in hair the color of golden wheat, tied back at the nape of his neck—barely cleared the low exposed beams of the ceiling. Dark-brown eyes highlighted a large, angular face. No doubt the man had Viking in his DNA.

As if used to being completely ogled, he crossed his arms and waited. Kat wasn't about to disappoint. Her brain cataloged biceps straining the weave of his cobalt-blue sweater. Jeans hugged thighs she could probably bounce rocks off of and led to chocolate-brown boots with some scrollwork she couldn't make out.

Dragging her gaze back up, she met his smile and

gripped the edge of the table to stop from fanning herself. The damn man even had dimples.

Heat and awareness battled along every inch of her body. This man oozed some type of "take me now" pheromone. She'd been instantly attracted to men before, but this modern-day Viking had infiltrated every nerve of her body. It didn't help that his eyes had done their own quick perusal and deepened in a bit of appreciation.

Knowing it would be rude to continue staring and even ruder to ask him to turn around so she could check out the view from behind, she smiled. "Did you need something?"

His arms dropped, and he cocked his head. "That's my table. See, big man." He poked himself in the chest. "Big chair."

Kat's gaze darted to the large sturdy seat he pointed at, different from all the other chairs in the café, then looked around, ignoring the fact that every other patron stared at them. She made a big show of moving her things into the middle of the table and even bent to look underneath it.

"I'm sorry. I don't see anything proclaiming this anyone's table."

Someone snickered behind her, and she narrowed her eyes despite the butthead not being able to see it.

"You don't know who I am, do you?"

"No." And she didn't really care, well at least not that much. She needed to fix her book, not engage in some territorial battle with a Viking.

Bella Harris hurried over. The owner of Beans and Leaves, the little café and coffee house, had started an uneasy get-to-know-you sort of friendship with Kat. Of course, this was only the third time she'd made it down the mountain since she'd moved to Colorado two months ago, so they were still in the put-your-best-foot-forward stage. Somehow, she imagined she'd stumbled back a few steps.

"Kat, honey, this is Trent Hawkins."

Mr. Hawkins flashed a smile and made a bow. "At your service."

It occurred to Kat that the name should mean something, and as she continued to glance around, it became even more obvious that some minor deity had entered her home away from home.

"Nice to meet you, Mr. Hawkins."

"Trent."

Bella glanced between her, Mr. Viking and the table, and after the third pass, Kat sighed. "You seriously want me to move?"

Bella's eyes widened, and she wrung her hands in the Escher print apron around her neck. A wave of guilt flowed through Kat leaving her weary and weak. It probably wasn't Bella's fault that she'd asked. Godlings tended to rant and rave till they got their way, at least in her experience. She would move for Bella's sake. No sense causing problems for a local business owner because an oaf of a man *needed* his table.

Bella touched her shoulder. "I'm sorry. It's just that he's already broken three of my chairs. This was the arrangement we came to. I feed him, and he leaves my furniture intact."

Kat managed a smile and shifted her notebooks into a pile. She didn't bother pointing out that they could have just moved the chair. She would like to be able to show her face in here again. It was the one place she could count on a steady internet connection, along with semi-peace and quiet.

The table shifted in her direction, and a quick glance showed Mr. Hawkins settling in across from her.

"No need to move. I'm fine sharing if you are."

Bella smiled. "I'll be back with your usual."

Kat narrowed her gaze again, but her scowl bounced off a ducked blond head. If he thought he would intimidate her, he was sadly mistaken. She had three brothers. She could outwit and outlast them all.

Hoe your own row.

Yeah, why should she leave a perfectly good table? She was here first, dammit. She could care less about any ranting and raving, as long as Bella's business and furniture weren't hurt.

Reacquainting herself with the Swiss cheese on the screen in front of her, she'd managed to plug a small hole when Bella returned with three huge plates and a carafe of coffee. Blondie, or rather Mr. Hawkins, smiled, picked up his fork, blew a kiss to Bella—who practically melted into the floor—and dug in. Kat stared mesmerized as he forked bite after bite of apple cinnamon pancakes into his mouth. Each movement was restrained with controlled energy. Next, he moved on to the omelet, and when a particularly cheesy piece fought to get into his mouth, his pink tongue swooped out and captured it.

Lord, no wonder everyone wants to worship this guy.

"I'm sorry, did you want some?"

Closing her eyes in mortification, she wondered if it was really possible to self-combust. Because this would be the perfect time for a quick exit. A chuckle reached her and, thankfully, flushed the mortification out of her system, replacing it with mild indignation.

Cocky. That was what sat across from her. A cocky, too-damn-good-looking-for-his-own-good man. She knew the type. Hell, she'd almost married the type. And this one apparently expected the entire female population to bow down at his feet. Well, she'd never been very skilled at bowing to begin with, so disappointment would reign from his side of the table.

"Need some more help with your grammar?"

Kat slammed down the lid of her laptop. "No. Thank you."

Her abrupt movement sent several pieces of paper flying, mostly toward blondie. His massive hands stopped the papers' escape, and he gathered them up, tapping them against the table to make them nice and neat. When he extended them the way-too-short distance toward her, she grabbed hold and managed a "thank you."

Only he didn't release them. She met his gaze and he smiled, deploying the dimples. "Now say it like you mean it."

"You know what? Keep them. They're not helping me anyway."

She shoved her things into her tote and reached for her leather journal.

"Hey, sorry. You don't have to leave. I was just having fun and trying to diffuse some of the tension, but clearly today is not the day to mess with you or your grammar and punctuation." He slid the papers across to her and leaned back in his chair, corded biceps clasped behind his head.

"So, what do you write?"

"Romance."

The legs of the chair slammed to the ground. "Romance?"

She froze. "Yes. Romance. Have a snide comment about that too?"

"Actually, no. I tend to not comment on things I don't know about. Learned the hard way that it leads to trouble. I've never read one, so it would be immature of me to speak about it."

Kat's mouth fell open. Man, if only half the talk pieces written about her chosen profession had taken his approach, the world might actually know some facts about the romance industry and its billion-dollar place in publishing. Instead, lazy reporters threw names like Fabio and terms like "bodice rippers" around like confetti. Of course, she and her fellow romance writers put up pretty darn good fights when those talk pieces got it wrong. But just once it might be nice to see them get it right.

Digging around in her other bag, she produced a copy of her first book. "Here. On me. I hope you like it."

She gathered the rest of her paraphernalia and stood.

"You're published."

"Yes, why?"

"Well…" He waved his hand toward the closed laptop. "The grammar."

She leaned down, hands on the table, and through a clenched jaw said, "It's going through edits."

"Ahhh."

She closed her eyes and counted to twenty. Ten was not cutting the bullshit factor across from her. When she was back in control of her temper, she opened her eyes only to see him already knee-deep in chapter one.

"You're reading it?"

Blondie arched an eyebrow. "Were you expecting me to use it as a paperweight or something?"

Kat collapsed back into the chair. "Yes. I mean no. Not exactly a paperweight, but I didn't expect you to read it."

"Why not? I like learning things. And who knows, maybe I'll learn a thing or two about…" He flipped back to the cover. "K. Monroe." He glanced up. "A pseudonym?"

She nodded, and the moment froze as she drowned in chocolate-brown eyes. Her body once again perked up, ready to tackle this Viking warrior. If she was half the writer she thought she was, she would have taken notes. It was the set up. The moment when two people were more aware of each other as a unit than as separate entities. The moment when someone's heart says, "Hey, dude, you may be something I need."

Her book needed those moments. She didn't.

"Well, enjoy."

Kat stood and brushed by him toward the door. The moment the Decker Springs air slapped her in the face with its crispness, she heard, "I think I really *am* going to enjoy it."

Trent shut his front door and dropped his keys into the ceramic bowl on the side table. His niece had made it for him, and although the intention had been bowl-like, he was pretty sure a wedge was a more apt description. Regardless, it was in his team colors and one of his most prized possessions.

As if thinking of his sister's offspring conjured her, his phone buzzed, and a quick glance showed a text.

Dinner. Tomorrow. Don't be late.

Smiling, he fired off a *Yes, ma'am* and headed to the kitchen. Breakfast was wearing off, and in its wake came that slow, gnawing hunger. If he didn't take care of it now, it would result in him whipping up a batch of cupcakes and then eating the whole two dozen. Wouldn't do to wreck his weight in the off-season. Although was this really the off-season anymore?

He had a few weeks to decide. Should he go out on top, or should he continue, knowing he wasn't getting any younger or happier? Seven years as a professional athlete had taken its toll physically, and honestly, playing the role required of him was wearing him down mentally. He sighed. Either way, thinking about it on an almost-empty stomach wasn't the wisest choice.

Assembling the salad took minutes. Everything in his fridge was prepackaged and easy to access for moments like this. His motto for alone time had been assess the weakness and turn it into a strength or block it at the pass.

Sweets were a weakness, and since turning gorging-on-sugar into a strength wasn't happening, he blocked the damn pass as often as he could. The baking supplies were on the top shelf behind boxes of granola and other healthier choices. The cookie sheets and pie plates rotated rooms. And his mixer was currently stashed in the garage.

Trent slid onto a barstool but jumped back down to remove something from his pocket. The book his lovely table stealer had given him. He'd already consumed five chapters, and while not Kafka (and really who was?) it was pretty good. A little tension, a little laugh, and a little intrigue. She definitely had some chops. Although by the look of her laptop, it took a lot to get her from start to finish.

Dropping the paperback onto the counter, he consumed the salad and debated what to bring to his sister's tomorrow night. Wine was a given, but he liked to bring something edible, since whatever she was serving usually wasn't. And of course, he needed something for his niece, Tilly.

His gaze traveled back to the cover of the book. Nice colors, catchy title.

K. Monroe.

The name bounced around him leaving warm spots wherever it touched. Bella had called her Kat, no doubt the extension of the *K*, and boy had she been a surprise. Something that didn't happen much these days. And if he was being truthful, the dismissive way she dealt with him had turned him on. The red hair, green eyes, and full, rounded figure hadn't been too shabby either.

Strong women were another weakness, one he might have to block at the pass. So, what was her scheme? Intrigue him by dismissing him?

He couldn't remember the last time a woman hadn't practically salivated on him. He didn't enjoy it, well at least not that much. Everybody liked having some adoration, but with his job, his profile, it came with the territory. Along with every conniving character known to man. It was hard knowing who to trust to see *him* and not Professional Football Player in big shiny lights.

Gathering his dishes, he loaded them in the dishwasher and leaned against the counter. No. He understood people, and she was seriously just perturbed by him. She had looked her fill but apparently found what he offered up to be lacking.

And that made him want to see her again.

Bad idea. Women had hardly been on his radar over the course of his career and especially not now with his future so up in the air. Not only was his job demanding both on and off the field—it would take a special kind of woman to handle that—but being in the spotlight made it hard to trust others. He'd been burned once by a woman who had seen the fame and not the man, and it had made him very cautious.

Still…

Grabbing the book, he went into his office and picked up his tablet. He settled into the leather chair in the corner and keyed in a few things and came across her website. Five minutes later, he had learned nothing except that she wrote books, loved her dog, and craved sweets. It didn't even mention that she lived around here, which, if he thought about it, made sense. But the fact that she didn't seem to know him, coupled with the fact that he didn't know her, led him to believe she'd moved to Decker Springs sometime during the season.

And he knew who to ask for the important details. Bella.

Violins pierced his thinking, and a quick glance at his phone showed his sister's number.

"Tasha, what's up?"

"Are you bringing anyone?"

"What?"

"Anyone. Do I need to set another place? Plan for vegan or tofu or something like that?"

Trent laughed. "Tash, have I ever just sprung a guest on you before?"

"No. But you aren't you. I mean, you've been distracted, understandably, and I wouldn't put it past you to have had a girlfriend for the past nine months and forget to mention her or her eating habits to me."

"No girl. No extra place. And for god's sake, don't ever mention tofu again."

"Love ya."

"You too. See ya tomorrow."

Chapter 2

Kat straightened the third blanket over her lap and adjusted her fingerless gloves. Mountain living wasn't for the faint of heart or the thin of skin, both of which she seemed to be. Maybe she should have considered that before buying this place. She blamed it partially on her warm Florida upbringing. Still, it was peaceful and occasionally inspirational, and cheap. Three criteria high on her life's list these days. A life created on a whim when her book had sold and she'd left her fiancé at the altar.

A life that needed some added income. Savings and a cashed-out 401k only went so far, even with smart investing.

She'd definitely broken one of those unspoken author rules about giving up your day job when you sell your first book. And while she didn't miss running a bank branch, she did miss the steady income.

Still, whims could work out, couldn't they? She certainly couldn't have stayed in Florida with the way the press had begun to hound her again thanks to her ex-fiancé finding a new woman.

Kat had lost count of how many times she'd told someone she wished the new couple well. And she did. Just because she'd discovered too late that the side her ex showed her was the fake one and the side he showed the world was the real Chad Hemmings, didn't mean this new woman's judgement was so poor. Maybe she liked men who were rude to waitstaff and expected to be catered to. Maybe the way he treated her privately balanced the ugly parts out. Sadly, Kat figured out too late that it didn't balance for her.

A lump shifted beside her legs, and a moment later elfin ears worked their way out of the covers.

"Riley, either get down or sit still."

Her corgi hadn't taken a liking to the cold either, which she totally didn't understand given his fabulous fur coat. But then again, he was strange in all sorts of ways, so why not with weather too?

He hopped down, cast a disparaging look only corgis could pull off and waddled his way over to the fireplace. Three circles later, he settled and went to sleep.

"Lucky pooch."

Returning her focus to the words on the screen, she reread the meeting between her two main characters. It was lacking something. That was the note her wonderful editor had left. Of course, the "something" remained unnamed, but Kat had a good feeling tension and passion and likability would all suffice.

He's not realistic. There's no swoon. Remember what it was like to fall in love. To feel that pull. To meet someone and wonder.

Kat snorted as she remembered her editor's words. Apparently, she'd faked it well enough in the first book. Not surprising, since she'd lived the whirlwind fantasy she'd written. Her emotions had spilled upon the page as she'd been wined and dined by one of the richest men in the world. The happily-ever-after on the page had not been echoed in her life, and this second book was screaming failure in the biggest way. Of course her hero wasn't realistic. Was anyone in books? Wasn't that why people read them? To escape. To find something they might not see in everyday life. To hope.

And fall in love?? Pshaw. Kat and love were now two ropes that coiled parallel to one another but never intertwined. Another fallout from her failed almost-marriage and subsequent trashing in the tabloids. It was bad enough to have a man she thought she loved labeling her a gold digger, but to then have people she thought were friends do the same thing? How could someone be a gold digger if they didn't ask for any money? She'd actually signed a prenup for goodness' sake, but apparently tabloids didn't believe in things called facts.

Her body tensed at the betrayal. No, trust wasn't coming anytime soon—either in herself or in a man—so that translated to no relationships.

But boy did she miss the sex and the connection with someone else. It had been nine months since she'd left Chad at the altar.

"I can't marry you. I don't know who you are...who the real you is. I suspect it is someone I wouldn't like very much."

She shivered at the memory and adjusted the blankets again. Counting to ten, she released a breath and focused on her now. Two months ago, she'd moved to Decker Springs, practically an entire country away from the still-occasional news story about her, and she didn't regret the impulsive decision. At least not most of the time.

Nope. Her trip down memory lane just reinforced the "no love for her" edict, so that meant she would need to research. Binge watch Netflix. Scroll through social media posts. Something to help her capture the pull. The feelings.

Just because she'd fallen off the love wagon didn't mean she couldn't tap into all the emotions, both the good and bad, loaded inside of it.

Her phone gonged, and a quick glance showed a text from Bella with a picture of her journal.

Left this here. Have it behind the counter.

Kat sighed. She sent back her thanks and mentioned she would be there tomorrow to get it. Her journal must have been forgotten in the midst of escaping Mr. Big and Blond.

His deep voice filtered in. *I think I'm going to enjoy it.*

Lord, that man knew how to work a woman.

Kat sat up. Bella had practically melted at the man's feet. Her no-nonsense, efficient, settle-them-down-with-a-stare friend had gone mushy. Every other woman in the shop couldn't keep her eyes from him. And to be honest, neither could Kat. And all he'd done was try to get his table and eat some food.

Even now, some three hours later, she was able to recall every facet of him in minute detail. He was realistic. Well, in an I-married-a-prince sort of way. But he apparently had that pull. What if she did some firsthand research?

Riley sneezed and pulled Kat back into the here and now. How on earth was she to get up close and personal with Trent what's-his-name? He clearly was somebody important in this town. Although for what, who knew? Maybe he was a trust-fund baby.

Great. Just what I need to tangle with, another man with unearned money.

Ignoring the warning, she closed down a window and opened Google. She typed *Trent,* and the first name to join it was Hawkins. Not one-hundred-percent sure, she clicked, and damned if a mighty fine, practically nude picture of blondie didn't populate her screen. It was black-

and-white, and although the manliest part of his body was discreetly covered by a football, every other line, muscle cleft, dimple, and shadow could be dissected.

And boy was she dissecting.

He was beautiful. Even his broad forehead and wide cheeks chiseled to an angle spoke of marble beauty rather than coarse sexuality. And since she knew his voice and his restrained strength were coupled with a package like this, it was no wonder women melted. Hell, she needed to get rid of at least two of the blankets now.

A damn football player. That was what he was. A really good, like makes lots of money and endorses things, football player. No wonder she didn't know who he was. Despite having three brothers, she'd be lucky to name five football teams, let alone a specific player.

But I sure as hell am not going to forget him now, am I?

As she clicked through images and read article after article about Mr. Hawkins, linebacker extraordinaire, convictions settled deep in her bones. If anyone could provide the kind of hands-on research she needed to get this book into shape, it was him. A brief line in one of the articles showed he did, indeed, live in Decker Springs, and she guessed that Bella's was one of the places he habitually haunted. She also learned this was the off-season for him, and his future in football was uncertain. Maybe he would take pity on her and let her observe his daily life and all the swooning that accompanied it.

As if sensing her crazy-pants idea, Riley lifted his head, barked, and settled back down, one paw covering his nose.

Yeah, like a world-class athlete who apparently only got a couple of months off a year would take some rude, wouldn't-recognize-him-if-his-name-was-on-a-mugshot woman up on her offer to shadow him. Hell, if she even brought it up, he would probably have the local sheriff there faster than she could die of mortification.

No. Her inability to capture love and all its spoils was on her. Her inability to trust and extend herself to people was her burden—although, when those closest to you let you down your entire life, you built a backbone of resilience. No one ever lived up to the expectations she set, not even herself. So, she'd better start finding sources that were reliable and forget about blondie and his damn dimples.

Trent stood across the street and attempted to see through the mass of customers inside Beans and Leaves. It wasn't unusual for him to show up there two days in a row, but he did like to spread his patronage around the small town. He definitely couldn't do three days, so if Kat wasn't in there today, he wasn't about to waste an opportunity.

Although, the impatience flowing through all two hundred and forty-five pounds of him had his feet ready to jog across the two-lane street and barrel right in. Consecutive days be damned. Bella might raise an eyebrow—hell, she might even corner him and demand to know his angle —but she wouldn't do much beyond that. They'd been friends since middle school, and she'd kept him grounded on more than one occasion.

A flash of red caught his eye, and relief weighed his limbs down. Kat strode purposefully down the sidewalk, her coat a shocking scarlet color that highlighted everything about her hair and skin and gave her determined movements even more of a spark. That spark called to him. Had him counting to one hundred in Latin and then following a path that led to her.

The door mooed as he pushed through it, and the patrons still gracing the café looked up, perked up, and smiled. He gave a general wave and noticed in an instant that Kat was engaged with the proprietor and his table was free. Sliding into the vacant seat, he clasped his hands behind his head and waited. Bella glanced over Kat's shoulder and narrowed her gaze, but she quickly returned to the woman who had caught his interest. Bella handed something to Kat, who hugged her and turned.

Widened eyes and a slight blush was all the encouragement Trent needed. He stood, smiled, and motioned to the chair across from him. Kat glanced between him and the seat several times. Her lips moved, although no sound could be heard. Finally, she came to some agreement with herself and nodded, walking over and dropping into the chair.

"Fancy seeing you here. Although from the way you fought for this table yesterday, I suppose I shouldn't be surprised. Bella said you normally rotate through Decker Springs establishments."

Trent let the fact that she'd asked about him warm his heart. She might be wary of him—in fact, he got the impression she was perturbed that he affected her in any way—but he knew the value of focusing on small victories.

Damn any small victories. I shouldn't be celebrating any victory regarding this woman or any other. I'm losing sight of this off-season. I need to figure out my football future, then I can focus on my personal one.

"When I'm here I like to visit several places, all with sturdy chairs of course." He winked. "But yesterday proved so enjoyable, I hoped to repeat it."

"Bella's food is delicious."

"As are her patrons. Are we working today? Fixing those grammar errors?"

She sat back and crossed her arms. "What was your name again?"

"Trent."

"And are you a writer, Trent? Degree in English lit? Perhaps a teacher?"

"Nope. Today, I'm a reader." He pulled out her paperback and settled back in the chair.

Bella dropped a plate in front of her along with a tea pot. "Eat up before you leave. I know you're not eating enough up on that mountain of yours."

Kat opened her mouth to say something, but snapped it shut.

Trent swallowed a smile. Kat had clearly learned that one didn't fight Bella when she thought you needed to eat. A quick narrowed glance at him, and Kat prepared her tea and snagged a bite of the Danish in front of her. Another quick glance, and she opened up whatever Bella had handed her and ran her finger down a column.

Trent eyed the spitfire redhead over the edge of the book. Did she really not know who he was? His knack for sizing up people had come as a bonus from reading and reacting to the front line. She hadn't shown anything to lead him to believe she was playing a game, but didn't everyone have an ulterior motive?

He dropped his stare a moment before her eyes lifted. Even through the pages of her book, he could feel the puzzlement and consternation. Her gaze floated over him leaving little pockets of awareness. He ruffled her. And he liked that he did.

They sat in silence for all of three minutes before her finger drumming reached through his focus. Her eyes were fixed on the window behind his shoulder, and once again her mouth moved although he couldn't quite make out the one-sided conversation.

"Use you for research."

That he heard. He leaned forward and stared. "What did you say?"

She sat up straighter and met his confused expression with confidence. "I want to use you for research. To find out what it is that makes women fall at your feet."

Trent picked up his mug and brought it to his lips but didn't drink. Inside he was screaming, "What the hell?!" This stunning, fascinating woman wanted to spend time with him. Get to know what made him irresistible. That intrigued him even more.

Only she didn't find him that way. It was purely scientific, if her matter-of-fact demeanor said anything.

Talk about a nice lure on a hook.

He tried to project boredom, as if every day a woman offered something like this to him. Inside, he was pure chaos. Arguments and temptation bouncing off one another, fighting for the right to answer.

"Just what kind of research did you have in mind?"

"Not that kind."

Laughing at the firm chin and pointed stare probably wouldn't score him any answers, so he responded with an arched eyebrow and waited.

"I'm apparently lacking a certain something in this book and am under a strict deadline. And since it appears you just have to breathe to get half the female population to sigh and flutter their lashes, I figured maybe following you around would help me determine what I'm missing. The book's due in two weeks. That's all I'm asking for. Maybe even less if you're as good as you seem to be."

"You want to follow me around?"

She nodded.

"For research."

A slower nod this time.

Well, if she was trying a new and novel approach to hooking him, she was definitely succeeding. He rocked onto the back two legs of his chair and consulted his gut. Which had only been wrong once in his entire life. She seemed sincere in her words. No warning bells. In fact, he still didn't know if she knew who he was.

"Do you really not know who I am?"

A blush spread like wildfire across the bridge of her pert nose, freckles jumping out in contrast. "I didn't yesterday, but I do now."

Hmm, what exactly did she know? Easy enough to find out, and again, he believed she told the truth. Although it was obvious she was aware of his magnetism, he couldn't detect anything other than curiosity. It seemed she really did just want to research him.

And he didn't know how he felt about that.

Only one way to find out. He definitely wanted to spend more time with her, and this seemed like a good excuse.

He dropped the chair back to the ground, startling her and bringing her attention back to his face.

"Sure. Be ready at five. I'll pick you up."

"What?"

Trent stood and pushed in his chair. "I have dinner plans tonight. I figure the best way to start this partnership is to jump in feet first, right? Now, if you'll excuse me, I have an appointment."

"Wait." She gathered her stuff. "Why can't I start now?"

He shrugged. "It's for a massage, but hey, I'm game if you are."

Her deepening blush was a balm to his soul. She might not be as immune to him as she seemed.

"No. That's fine. Tonight's good. It will allow me to get

my thoughts and questions in order." She scribbled some-thing and ripped it out of her notebook. "There's my address."

He read it and his brows rose. "You're living up at the old Smighten place?"

Her spine straightened. "Yes, why?"

The tempting woman had just risen about ten notches on his find-out-more meter. The old Smighten place was up a one-lane mountain road that in the winter was practi-cally unnavigable. He'd heard the old man had passed, and he'd just assumed the house would sit unused. Why would a woman like this, who brightened every room she entered, resign herself to living a mountain-man existence?

Strength.

The determined looks, the quick wit, and the I'm-not-backing-down demeanor all combined into a package of strength and capability. No one with anything but those traits could handle living on the mountain.

"No reason. Be ready at five."

Chapter 3

What had seemed like a sensible plan three hours ago now seemed like the most foolish move she'd ever come up with. Well, next to almost marrying Dumbass McGee.

"Follow you around for research." Could she have sounded any more desperate? Trent Hawkins probably assumed she wanted a booty call and would show up here expecting one. If so, would he be in for an awakening. This two-week thing was strictly business. It didn't matter that everything about him screamed seven minutes in heaven. She didn't trust her judgement in men, especially men like him. No, she would set him straight if he even hinted at a booty anything, and she would totally have backup in the form of her clothes, which screamed "abominable snow-man" not "take me now, linebacker."

Laughter erupted, starting deep in her belly. It wasn't the first time she'd found it hysterical that she wrote romance for a living and had never truly experienced the imaginative sex scenes she created out of thin air. Simple could be nice, but a girl could use a little extra now and then. Not that she was planning on any "extra" with her research subject, but if Trent did read her book, he was going to get a glimpse into one of her more interesting scenarios.

She needed to cool down and focus on business, not picture the linebacker reading the outdoor scene that started on page 106.

What was a linebacker anyway? She hadn't explored beyond the whole football player thing. Should she know more about his position?

As she shook her head, her ponytail slipped loose, and her hair fell in front of her face. Blowing it out of the way, she reinforced the no. She needed to know what it was about him that made him irresistible to the women around him. Knowing about the position he played probably didn't equate to much.

Riley sat up and rumbled a low growl. A half second later his bread-loaf body waddled away, and it was apparent her visitor had arrived. Shoving her notebook and pen into her satchel, she raced to the door, hoping to beat Trent to the doorbell. The sound sent Riley into a frenzy that took ten minutes to wear off.

But just as the door clicked open, the bell pealed through the house. Riley took it upon himself to change up the banshee routine and squeeze his rotund little body through an opening she could have sworn wasn't big enough.

As Trent whirled around trying to follow the blur of tri-colored fur, Kat screamed, "Riley, get back here!"

Kat brushed past her visitor, ignoring the rock-hard chest her elbow traced. She cleared the small porch just in time to see her damn dog bolt for the tree line.

"Oh god, I'll never get him back."

A shrill whistle pierced the clearing, birds scattering into the sky.

Kat turned wide eyes on her visitor, who had chosen to destroy her eardrums. But just as quickly, Riley came trotting up and sat on Trent's foot.

"Good dog." He bent down and scooped her canine companion up, exposing his belly. "Do you like belly rubs, Riley?"

Riley's head lolled over Trent's corded forearm, his tongue hanging out as belly rubbing bliss took over, sending him into euphoria.

Lucky dog.

"You might want to shut your mouth. Who knows what kind of bugs will accept the invitation up here."

Kat snapped her mouth shut and crossed her arms. "How?"

"Believe it or not, my sister, Tasha, has a corgi also. Daisy has a knack for bolting, but always comes for the whistle. I figured I had nothing to lose."

"Except my hearing."

"Excuse me, was that a thank you?" He winked. "You're welcome."

Kat reached for her dog who fought tooth and nail to stay in the comfortable arms of the man who made her feel out of sorts. "Traitor," she whispered as she carried Riley inside.

"I wouldn't be too hard on him. I hear I give good belly rubs."

Kat almost dropped the damn dog. She bet he did give good belly rubs. *Maybe I could find out. You know, in the name of research.*

"I have no doubt you're skilled at a good many things, Mr. Hawkins."

"Aww man, you're using my formal name." He held his hand out in a plea. "I'm sorry I made your dog like me."

She dropped Riley on the couch and snagged her satchel. Finally meeting his gaze, she couldn't contain the shock of allowing herself to really look at him. Sure, she'd ogled him at the coffee house, but here, in her space, her home... He filled it. Encompassed it. Fit as if the space was designed for him.

Tall, bulky in places she liked bulk. Silky blond hair pulled back at his neck. Chocolate-brown eyes waiting, searching, and doing a fine job of making her believe they liked what they saw.

Viking indeed, maybe with a little mountain man thrown in for good measure.

Keeping it strictly business was going to be harder than she thought.

He's a public figure. One who plays roles. Roles fostered distrust. Distrust destroyed relationships. Not. For. You.

"Thank you for helping with Riley." Her voice came out wispy, and she took a deep breath and broke eye contact. This was bad. Really bad. Like, she'd just pictured Trent up in her bedroom reliving the naked magazine spread bad.

She should back out. History showed she couldn't trust her judgement, especially with charismatic men like Trent Hawkins.

His charisma, however, is exactly what I need to convey in the book. What's missing.

"You're welcome."

His response was gravelly, and she chanced a glance to see him examining her desperately needed-to-be-shampooed carpet.

"Well, we should go. I think. I mean we don't want to be late, right?" she stammered.

"Right…" He turned and walked to the door.

"I can follow you."

Trent spun on his heel, and Kat managed to avoid plastering herself up against him.

So close.

"Don't be crazy. I can drive us and bring you back."

This was entering dangerous territory on more than one level. It was entering pseudo-date territory.

"Mr. Hawkins, I'm more than…"

He held up a finger to her lips, silencing her on a gasp. "I know you're capable and smart and a whole host of other things. But if I recall, you asked to research me. I would think my driving skills would rank up there. I mean who finds an asshole driver appealing?"

He was talking. Words were coming out, and all Kat noticed was the warmth of the finger against her lips. How liquid her whole body had become. From a single touch. How was she even still standing?

If she could manage to transfer half of this onto the page, her editor would be offering her a three-book contract.

Riley barked, and she stepped back. "Fine, you drive."

Trent had never been more thankful for a game face and big-ass truck than he was at this moment. Kat sat in the passenger seat, a huge console separating them. Her red hair covered her shoulders, creating a fiery veil. Everything about Kat spoke to fire and backbone. He'd taken things too far at her house. Saving her dog, insisting on driving. Touching her silky lips. But he hadn't felt like having another battle. She was independent, he got that. No one moved to the old Smighten place who didn't plan on doing things their own way. But it was the vulnerability underlying the strength that piqued his interest.

Well, that and she was just downright stunning in other ways too. Even her voice flowed around him looking for a way in. Add to that, he knew all about her most intimate desires—or he supposed he did, thanks to her book—and Kat was a package tailor-made to make him forget about the important decisions he needed to make and drop everything for a wild fling. His past and current uncertain future meant there was no way it could be anything more than a fling, but he knew it would be one heck of a ride.

Nope. Not going to happen. She had an agenda and so did he. She had a book to finish, and he had a football future to sort out. Spending time with her was just that. Time.

"So, where are we going?" She asked the question to the scenery passing by, and he didn't blame her. She was fully aware of how much attraction flared between them, and since she'd clearly decided to ignore it, that made his battle slightly less difficult.

"My sister's."

"What?" she shrieked.

Her panic swirled around the truck and made breathing slightly *more* difficult.

"My sister. Standing dinner on the off-season."

"I'm going to your family's."

"No," he shot back, taking a turn wider than he'd planned on. "I'm going to my family's. You're tagging along. For research."

"Oh."

He couldn't risk a glance, but he could picture the erotic shape her luscious full lips were sporting on that simple word.

The rest of the ride was silent. Normally, Trent

relished quiet time for his thoughts. Some of his best ideas came from car rides, his goals forming crystal clear in the silence of his cab. But this silence was uneasy. Like he'd agreed to more than he actually had. Like by stepping into Kat's world, and she into his, they had upended something in the realm of fate and now all bets were off.

Thankfully, his sister's cabin came into view just as the tension was becoming unbearable.

"How adorable."

The glee on Kat's face was worth the awkwardness. Trent hadn't accomplished everything he had in life by letting fate lead. He made his own way, and there was nothing stopping him from sidestepping fate now.

"I'll be sure to tell Tasha you approve."

"No. No, I didn't…"

"I was kidding."

"Oh."

Don't look. Don't look.

Kat opened the door before Trent even had a finger on the handle of his door. He normally opened a lady's door —after all, his mother, God rest her soul, raised him to be a gentleman—but it was probably for the best with this particular woman that he not. Their lines were already shaded in all sorts of gray and she hadn't even been shadowing him for two hours. No sense tempting any more fate bombs.

He hopped out, grabbed a bag off the back seat and circled the back of the truck, but before he could offer any info on what Kat was stepping into, the front door opened.

"Uuunnncle Trrreeennnt."

A banshee with white-blond hair and crystal-blue eyes came racing up to him full-blown. He put the bag on the ground and caught her midleap, swinging her around much to the delight of the giggling girl.

In the middle of the spin, he caught the grin and joy on Kat's face. The longing she couldn't disguise if she'd worn a mask, spilling over every line of her peaches-and-cream complexion.

He set his niece down and grabbed the little girl's hand. "Tilly, this is my friend Kat." He looked at his voluptuous shadow. "We're all *T* names in case you hadn't caught on."

Tilly jutted out her hand. "It's nice to meet you, Kat. Uncle Trent never brings friends over to play."

Kat shook her hand. "Well, I love to play, so you name it and I'm game."

And just like that, Trent was relegated to second string. A place he hadn't been since his early junior high days.

He led the new BFFs into his sister's house, even more uneasy over the blurred lines developing between he and Kat.

"Trent, it's nice of you to be on—" His sister's mouth dropped open as he stepped to the side revealing the two peas in a pod. He shrugged sheepishly and hoped to god Tasha wouldn't out him.

"Welcome to our home. I'm so glad you were able to join us."

"Hi, I'm Kat Evans."

His sister moved past him strategically jabbing a bony elbow into his ribs as she muttered, "She better not expect tofu."

Before Tasha could envelop her guest in a hug, her canine sidekick barreled its way down the hall and planted two paws on Kat's thighs.

She squealed and dropped to the floor. "Oh, Trent mentioned you had a corgi. I have one named Riley." Kat buried her face in the fur and crooned.

"Well, we'll have to get Riley and Daisy here together."

Kat beamed. "I would love that. I haven't had a chance to get to know too many other residents in town yet."

Trent rubbed the back of his neck, unable to get the genuine smiles out of his vision. Kat had already piqued his interest. Kat grinning like she'd won the lottery wiped all traces of anything sane from his mind.

Left once again to his own devices, he stepped into the kitchen only to freeze. What on god's green earth had his sister attempted to cook this time?

"Oh, I love brussels sprouts and artichokes," Kat said behind him.

Even Trent, only knowing Kat for a short time, knew she was being polite. Her voice, normally a deeper husky tone, was high-pitched and as fake as the flowers sitting in the middle of his sister's dining room table. Not that it should come as a shock. Who honestly liked brussels sprouts and artichokes?

"Is there meat, Tash?"

His sister shot him the glare of death and quickly turned back to Kat. "Of course there's meat. I made beef Wellington."

Kat smiled. "My grandmother used to make that once a month on Sundays."

Trent crossed the room and handed his sister the bag with the bottle of wine and the flan he'd brought. "Can't wait to eat, Sis."

"Yes, well why don't you take Kat out to the deck where the appetizers are. Pete's on a business call, he'll be out in a few."

He guided his guest to the French doors keeping the touch on her lower back as light and simple as possible. Her perfume, which had filled his nostrils in the truck, now wafted in tantalizing snippets that begged him to lean forward and find out where the concentration was the highest.

His hand dropped as if it was a dumbbell and he'd finished a final set. This was all sorts of madness. He was in his sister's house for god's sake. How many times did he have to remind himself that he had no place in his life for a woman right now? Especially one who apparently liked her isolation. He had a decision to make about his future and football. A decision with a deadline. Ironically a deadline that mirrored his research time with Kat, minus a day. If he kept playing, his life was not conducive to relationship and definitely not with a woman who liked living on a mountain. Not to mention, as much as he was starting to like her and was attracted to her, they'd known each other for a day. Trust was not something built in twenty-four hours.

Women with him had to endure the spotlight, and that was hard even for the strongest of people. If he decided to retire, he didn't know where his life might be heading. Either option was a fumble waiting to happen when it came to a relationship.

"Your niece obviously adores you."

"Why wouldn't she?" He shrugged. "I spoil her rotten, give her candy, tell her all her dreams will come true, and basically worship the ground she twirls on."

"So you lie."

Trent didn't miss the underlying strain to her statement. "I encourage."

She didn't look convinced. "I think you're setting her up for failure."

"Failure's part of life."

"Don't I know that." Her hand snapped up and covered her lips on that oh-so-alluring "oh."

Confessions spilled out of her like lava from an

erupting volcano. She resembled one too, with her long, flowing red hair.

"Sorry."

"Hey, no need to apologize. Life sucks."

"Says the rich football player whose dreams came true."

"How do you know what my dreams are and if they came true or not?"

She looked absolutely apologetic as she said, "You're right. We're strangers. Our dreams don't come into play. Only your animal magnetism."

He slung an arm across her shoulder, the warmth of her body spreading down his side and settling like it had found a home. "I like the sound of that."

Chapter 4

KAT SOAKED UP ALL THE MEMORIES SHE COULD AS SHE
dried the plate Tasha handed her. Memories from tonight
would have to be enough because she was already in so far
over her head that there could be no more research of Mr.
Hawkins. He was like every fantasy man ever created, in
flesh and blood. He looked like a god, loved his family,
swallowed bites of horrid food while complimenting his
sister on her culinary skills. He currently danced with his
niece outside after completing a game of catch with her
and his brother-in-law. Short of Trent trying to correct her
grammar and maybe being a little extra cocky, she could
find no fault with him.

Danger, Will Robinson.

Yes, she needed help. But if she continued spending
time in Trent Hawkins's bubble, the kind of help she'd
need would be for mending a broken heart.

"So, what do you do, Kat? Trent didn't mention."

Kat slid the dish into the cabinet. "I'm a writer."

"Ooh, what kind?"

Kat tensed and said, "Romance."

Tasha dropped a dish back into the sink. "Do you know Kristan Higgins?"

Relief flowed through her and she laughed. "Not personally."

"Oh, well I love her. I would love to read one of your books."

"Trent has one."

Tasha's eyes rose to the ceiling. "Does he now?" She canvassed Kat's face several times. "Just how long have you and my brother been dating?"

Kat sputtered and had to put down the glass she was drying. "We're not. Dating, I mean. I'm using him for research."

That sent Tasha into huge belly laughs. "Is that what they're calling it these days?"

Trent chose that moment to come inside. "And what are you two giggling about?"

Kat wanted to point out that nothing on her face resembled laughter, but that would only invite more questions.

Tasha wiped her eyes. "Kat tells me she's using you for"—she made air quotes—"research."

Trent crossed his arms, and Kat let herself visually trace his chest. Just how wide was it?

"She is," he said matter-of-factly.

That just sent another wave of laughter through Tasha until both her husband and daughter came into the kitchen wondering what had happened to her.

Kat crossed her arms too and met Trent's eyes with a smirk. He shrugged. At least the two of them understood the relationship. The professional relationship. The one she would break off tonight. Why oh why hadn't she driven herself? She could have already made a break for it and been back in her freezing house with the memories.

"Tasha, I think it's time Kat and I hit the road. We have an early start tomorrow, and she lives up at the old Smighten place."

That stopped Tasha in her tracks. "Are you crazy?"

"No. At least, I don't think I am."

"Is that place even inhabitable?"

"Of course. It's quaint and cozy."

"And a prime scene for a murder. Maybe you should switch genres."

"Tasha, that's enough. Kat has a lovely home, and she's a very capable woman."

Heat flushed her veins. On the one hand, she loved that he was defending her even if he accompanied it with an exaggerated wink. On the other hand, guilt thickened her throat. She really wasn't all that capable. Capable people didn't run from their problems to live on top of a mountain in, let's face it, the ideal setting for a horror movie.

"I'm sorry," Tasha offered sincerely. "I just wouldn't want anything to happen to you."

"I appreciate that, and I'm fine, honest." *Sorta. Maybe.*

Kat and Trent took their leave quickly after that, and before she knew it they were headed back to her house. The sun had slipped behind the Sawatch Range, and the trees were dark shadows against a pale sky. She'd always loved this time of night. When things seemed possible, magical. When the mystery was inviting, the details hidden.

But right now, sitting in the cab of a truck with the man of her book-dreams, she would give anything to not be thinking of magical possibilities involving him. Give anything to have the details be ugly rather than inviting.

On paper, Trent Hawkins could just be a different version of her almost-groom. He lived in the spotlight, someplace she swore she would never let herself be again, unless it was on her terms. She had no doubt he played a role part of the time and even if the man she witnessed tonight seemed genuine, how could she trust her judgment?

Still…

Magical possibilities.

Trent pulled up to Kat's house and shifted into Park.

"Thank you so much, Mr. Hawkins. Tonight was the perfect brand of research. In fact, I garnered so much that I think I'm good. I appreciate you taking the time out of your severely limited off-season to accommodate me."

Trent had read cues most of his life, and this one was coming across as a brush-off. And that sat about as well with him as the thought of eating more of Tasha's beef Wellington. They'd had a lovely evening. Kat had fit in with his family like she was made to be there. He'd thought, no he'd known, she'd had a fabulous time. So why the formal Mr. Hawkins and the need to cut things off just when they were getting started?

"Wow, and here I thought you were a thorough writer."

Her hand had been on the door handle, and now it was pointing right at his face. He loved being able to read people so well.

"I am thorough."

"But what about kissing?"

Her eyes widened, and she moistened her lips. "Kissing?"

"I mean that surely is something you would need to research, right?"

"I, uh. I mean a kiss is a kiss. Not much research in that."

Oh boy was Kat Evans wrong. A kiss was not a kiss, and he was going to enjoy every minute proving her wrong, in the name of research.

She chose his silence as agreement and opened the door. He exited also and circled around the front of the truck, following her up the small porch.

"What are you doing?"

"Walking you to your door."

"You don't have to do that."

He shrugged. "Just did. And now?"

"Now?"

Her keys were out but her head had tilted up to him, and her eyes held as many questions as the breathlessness in her voice.

He stepped closer and waited to see her response. She swayed toward him and he took another step and slid his arms around her waist. "Do you really believe a kiss is a kiss?"

She licked her lips again and nodded the slightest bit.

"You're wrong." Trent lowered his head. "Will you let me kiss you, Kat?"

She closed her eyes and whispered, "Yes."

He brushed his lips against hers in the lightest touch. His body urged him to move faster, claim her mouth and take control, but he knew better. This was the opposite of a blitz, and he was taking her down one nibble at a time.

She stepped closer, and he tightened his arms and tasted the corners of her mouth, alternating with his lips and tongue. Kat snaked a hand up his back and into his hair, and for a moment he forgot what his goal was. She took advantage and opened her lips, her tongue tracing his mouth, and before he knew it their tongues were engaged in a dance of passion as each pressed closer to the other. She was soft and warm in his arms, her curves fitting his like a lock and key. The inside of her mouth was like warm honey, and he couldn't get enough.

Scratching sounds invaded the sighs and moans they produced, and Kat pulled away. It took more willpower than the final rep on a 225 bench press to let her go. She broke contact and dropped her chin to her chest.

He kissed the top of her head. "Tomorrow. Please spend the day with me. I promise it's for a good cause, and you'll learn a lot. For the book, of course."

She squeezed him tight and broke free, refusing to meet his gaze. "Text me where." Then she slid through the door, shutting it after her.

He stared until a light flicked on, and he forced his feet to move toward his truck. He had been intent on showing her a kiss wasn't just a kiss, but Kat Evans hadn't been the only one learning a lesson on her porch.

The question now was, what to do with this newfound knowledge? Pursuing Kat for anything other than this two-week research stint was insane. His plan was just to spend time with her while he was back home figuring out his football future, not get caught up in something that could lead to more. Heck, he didn't even know where his life would be two weeks from now, let alone how a potential relationship would fit in.

Yet...

He rubbed the back of his neck and laughed. He may not know a whole lot about two weeks from now, but what he did know was that no man could experience the highest of highs from a simple kiss and not want to continue down that path.

Chapter 5

Kat applied the brakes and took a quick glance in the mirror. Nerves tickled her stomach, leaving her breathless and—not for the first time this morning—wondering what the hell a kiss had done to her normally reliable brain. Her plan had been to cut this off. No more research. Instead, one totally shoot-for-the-stars kiss had her agreeing to accompany Trent today.

The light changed, and she leaned forward, looking for the side street that would take her to Watkins Elementary. At least in the recesses of her kiss-fogged mind she'd managed to insist on driving herself. Close quarters with Trent Hawkins was a combination guaranteed to leave her addicted.

Five minutes later, she locked her car and glanced around for the mountain of a man she was supposed to be meeting.

"Kat."

She turned and her breath caught. Did the man look good in everything? He wore a T-shirt with the name of the elementary school stretched wide across his chest, and black athletic pants. She ran her hands down her jeans and thanked her lucky stars she'd gone causal. Crossing the lot to him, she ordered her body, brain, and heart to get in sync. This was research. Watch and learn. No touching, and for heaven's sake no more kissing.

He smiled and shoved his hands in his pockets. "I thought you might not show up."

"Trust me, so did I."

"I'm glad you did."

Research. Research. Dimples are overrated.

He waved her forward, and they fell into step. They were buzzed into an office where Kat produced her driver's license and received a visitor sticker to wear in return.

"Mr. Hawkins, so nice to see you again."

Kat turned to see an older woman with glasses on her head and a twinkle in her eye.

"You too, Mrs. Laughman. This is one of the highlights of my year."

"As it should be." She swatted his arm. "I mean, I didn't put up with your childhood antics for nothing."

Kat giggled.

"And who did you bring with you today?"

"Mrs. Laughman, may I present Kat Evans."

"It's nice to meet you, Mrs. Laughman. Thank you for letting me crash this little event."

The woman looked Kat up and down and nudged Trent. "I like this one."

Trent snorted. "Don't you dare. She's just studying me."

Kat's cheeks flooded with heat. The way *he* studied *her* should be criminal.

"Studying, huh?"

"I'm a writer. Mr. Hawkins is being kind enough to let me follow him around."

Mrs. Laughman grinned and nodded. "I see. Well, we certainly could use the help."

"Just don't put her in the grammar bowl," Trent said.

Mrs. Laughman laughed. "But she just said she's a writer."

"Don't you say another word, Mr. Hawkins, or you will appear in my next book, and I promise I'll devise a very painful death for your character."

"I *really* like her." Mrs. Laughman said and looped her arm through Kat's. She led her out into the school. Trent followed, a grin on his face.

They entered the auditorium and several kids noticed Trent. They made a beeline for him before any of them could be corralled. Kat stepped back and watched as he patted each on the head and answered their questions. Each one was given eye contact and undivided attention. Several teachers came up and escorted his little fans back to their seats, and Trent and Mrs. Laughman made their way up onto the stage.

Kat slid further along the wall until she was toward the back and out of sight as much as possible. When Trent spoke, the tenor of his voice reached across the huge room and slid along her skin. Memories of his voice from last night seeped in: *Will you let me kiss you, Kat?* She crossed her arms on a shiver that had nothing to do with the temperature.

"You cold?"

Kat turned to see another young woman beside her. She held a tablet in her hand, and although her eyes were glued to the perfect specimen of a man at the front of the room, it was clear she'd been speaking to Kat.

"No. I'm fine. Thank you."

The woman typed a few things on the tablet and then turned brilliant blue eyes her way. "I bet you are. How long have you been dating the hometown hero?"

"I'm not." Lord everyone in Decker Springs was drawing lines where there was no connection.

She snorted and typed some more. "Trent Hawkins has never brought a woman to anything in this town in his entire life."

"People can change, Ms.?"

"Rachael. Rachael Martin. *Rocky Mountain News.*"

A chill spread across her shoulders. A reporter. They were vultures circling for a nibble and Kat had stepped right into the scavenger zone. She should have expected it. Trent was a famous athlete, of course there would be press covering the event. Her vision narrowed…

Ms. Evans, how does it feel to be one of the most hated women in America right now? I mean you broke Chad Hemmings's heart at the altar. Didn't like having to sign a prenup? Being adored by one of the richest men in the country wasn't enough for you?

She forced the memories of her past away. Obviously, this wasn't her first rodeo with press looking for juicy gossip. If she could handle the tabloids at her most vulnerable, she certainly could handle a newspaper reporter. Straightening her spine, she faced the blond full on.

"Ms. Martin, I can assure you the only reason I am here today is to lend my support to the community and the school. Trent Hawkins is a good man and a great catch, but I don't have a line out."

***

Trent swung his arm down, the flag in his hand fluttering in the early spring breeze. He hadn't seen Kat for most of the morning, and the accompanying disappointment was something he probably should examine a bit closer. Five kids ran past him, their little arms pumping for all they were worth. One broke through the piece of tape and shook his fists in the air. Trent jogged over and high-fived him.

They only had two more field events left. The quiz bowl was going on in the auditorium with the finals set to start as soon as he finished up here.

"Mr. Hawkins?"

He plastered on his good-ole-boy grin and turned to greet the reporter from the *Rocky Mountain News*. Tessa Martin had been following his career almost as long as he'd had one. He'd seen her speak to Kat briefly when they first arrived, but Kat seemed to handle the sly reporter in stride.

"Tessa. How are things these days?"

"They'd be better if you'd give me the scoop about your future."

"What scoop?"

She flicked her ponytail back and laughed. "You're good. Almost as good as your girlfriend today."

Trent stepped back and let his hand drop again. Five more kids ran as if ravenous zombies were hot on their tail. "Have you started writing fiction, Tessa? Last I checked there was no special someone keeping me in line."

She stared at him far too long for his liking, but he'd faced down offensive tackles three times her size and not nearly as cheerful. Her probing was like the buzzing of an annoying gnat.

"Funny, Ms. Evans was much more blunt in her denial."

He kept the reaction internal, but it pricked and prodded his chest. Of course she would deny being his girlfriend. There was nothing between them. *Except a kiss and a connection that had me up half the night.*

"So, it seems you have your facts straight." He smiled and gestured for her to cross the track with him. "I promise if there's a story to tell, Tessa, you'll know it."

The reporter kept her silence all the way to the auditorium, but just before they parted she said, "You're the biggest news story in the off-season, and my gut is saying the story is about more than whether or not you retire." She went off to join the other media representatives in the far corner. Trent shook his head and then immediately looked for the fiery redhead he'd been thinking about way too much today.

He spotted her with a group of children, all showing off the medals they'd picked up during the day. She was congratulating them and sharing in their delight, and his chest tightened at the pure joy spilling from her face. Before he could help himself, he wondered how he could make her look at him the same way.

She looked up and at him and smiled. His feet carried him toward her without his brain making the decision to do so. The kids hurried to their seats as Mrs. Laughman clapped to get their attention.

"I see you found some fans."

"Actually, they're your fans, but maybe in a few years one or two could be mine."

"I missed you today." She sucked in a breath and he quickly clarified. "I mean, I didn't see you for most of the day. Probably not the greatest day for research."

Kat dropped her gaze. "I think I got a good picture without being by your side."

"Well, before I forget, here." He unfolded his hand and a medal dropped.

Fingers that trembled reached out and traced the medallion. She looked up with a question.

"Honorary, of course. Here let me."

He placed it over her head and straightened the twisted fabric in the back, his fingers brushing the silky skin of her neck. They were close and the whole school was watching, including a host of reporters who probably had every available camera aimed in their direction. That was the only thing that kept him from leaning forward and tasting her lips again.

The brightening green of her eyes and the quickening rise and fall of her chest told him she was just as affected as he.

They parted, and she picked up the medal. "Thank you."

He made his way to the front to take up his final duty of the day, but as he passed the media section, Tessa wiggled her fingers and said, "Definitely more to the story."

Chapter 6

Kat settled into her table and pulled out her laptop. The holes that had plagued her story were being filled at an alarming rate, and fleshing out her hero was coming too easily all of a sudden.

"Coffee or tea?" Bella asked as she set a white ceramic cup and saucer down in front of her.

"Tea, I think. Surprise me."

Bella returned a few minutes later with a glass jar of loose leaves, a steeper in the shape of a sloth, and hot water.

"I went with something different. You look like a woman on a mission."

Kat thanked her and prepared the tea. Hanging the sloth on the side of the mug, she smiled. She *was* on a mission. A mission to finish this book, get it to her editor by the deadline, and not fall for the handsome inspiration in the process.

As the cliché went, two out of three wasn't bad. Was it?

She jumped ahead to the scene where the hero and

heroine shared their first kiss. Memories flooded her, and she closed her eyes remembering the rush, the feel of Trent's lips. The way his body slid against hers, perfectly molding in all the right places.

"Your lips okay?"

Her eyes flew open to find Trent standing beside the table. "My lips?"

"Yeah, you were touching them with your eyes closed."

Lord, could she be any more embarrassed at this moment? "Ah, the tea was a little hot."

His gaze dropped to the mug in front of her, the sloth still hanging on the side with a cheery grin.

Nope, correct that. *Now* she couldn't be any more embarrassed.

He slid into the chair across from her. "So, how have you been?"

She removed the sloth and stirred in some honey. *Confused. Distracted.* "Good, and you?"

"Good. Just waiting."

"For what?" She stirred in sugar, then mentally smacked her forehead. She'd already sweetened with honey.

"For you."

The spoon dropped and clattered against the teacup. She stared, waiting for more details, praying they were ugly details, not the kind that would keep her up even later at night.

"Well, I hadn't heard from you. I mean, I didn't know if you needed anything specific for this research of yours, but surely we aren't done yet. My magnetism has infinite layers."

Do not think about it. Do not think about it. *Sex. Sex. Sex.*

"What do you mean?" She was proud that her voice

was even, considering her nerves were jumping and swaying for any chance to be close to him again.

"For the book. You know, did you need to see me doing anything specific?"

"Umm, not that I can think of."

"Maybe if I read it?"

"No!"

He cocked an eyebrow. "I read your other book. It was good."

Ignoring the swell of pride, she stammered, "But that was a finished product. This is not."

"Okay. Well then, if you're free, how about I cook dinner for you?"

"Cook?" *Wordsmith at it again.*

"Yes, cook. I can do that. I would think it might be something you'd want to research."

She couldn't for the life of her figure out why cooking would enter any woman's mind when sitting across from Trent Hawkins, but she grabbed onto the lifeline and held tight.

"Sure, sounds like a research plan."

"My place?"

Danger. Danger. Panic bolted through her nerves and she gripped the edge of her shirt under the table. She couldn't control things at his place.

"How about you come to mine? Riley hasn't gotten used to being left alone for long periods of time."

Trent smiled and was nice enough not to point out that she currently had left her dog alone. But then again, he didn't know how long she'd been in Beans and Leaves.

"Your place it is. Four sound good?"

"Little early for dinner, don't you think?"

"I have to prep before I cook."

She sighed. "Do you do everything well?"

He stood, and she followed his body up with her eyes. "Isn't that what your job is for the next eleven days? To uncover all my hidden talents."

She stared out the window long after Trent and his subtle challenge had left.

"Want me to heat up the water?"

Kat turned an embarrassed expression to her friend. "No. I think I've had enough hotness for one day."

"Girl, I don't think there will ever be too much hotness when it comes to Trent Hawkins."

Neither did Kat, and that was her biggest problem—wanting more of something suspiciously similar to what she'd run from. Trent Hawkins perfectly represented the celebrity boyfriend of people's dreams, with his charm and looks and good causes. She'd seen men like him in action, schmoozing. Her judgement with men like him was impaired at best.

Then again, Trent didn't schmooze. He talked and listened. He made eye contact, and each person seemed to leave an interaction with him as if they had been seen and heard and valued for however brief a time. Sure, he was cocky, but in a self-deprecating way, not an I-am-man-hear-me-talk kind.

See, this was her problem. While he was similar in many ways to what she'd fled, his underlying traits were different. He was true and kind and downright addicting...

Trent parked his truck and gripped the steering wheel. He'd had a phone call with his agent in the middle of the grocery store and the pressure to decide was mounting. It wasn't just the media circling, it was team members, publicists, managers. He understood. They needed to make a plan and they needed to know if he was a part of that plan.

Stretching his neck muscles, he closed his eyes and let the concerns fade away. Tonight was not about ten days from now, or a month from now, or even tomorrow. Tonight was a time for him and Kat. For her it might be research, but for him it was just an enjoyable evening between two people who liked one another.

He climbed out and grabbed the two bags of groceries off the passenger seat, along with a bouquet of flowers. Choosing flowers for Kat had taken longer than figuring out what to cook and buying the ingredients. He wanted something special for her because she deserved it. Something that represented the strength he admired in her. Something bold yet delicate.

He'd chosen dahlias. They were in a cascade of colors, long, strong stems supporting huge blooms, but each bloom was made up of a delicate swirl. They seemed a perfect representation of Kat Evans.

Trent heard Riley's barks and waited for the door to open. No sense tempting fate twice with the energetic pup. A minute later, the door opened to reveal Kat looking more beautiful than he had ever seen her. Her cheeks were flushed, her hair piled up on her head, exposing that graceful, made-for-kissing neck. She wore leggings, a long green open sweater, and a purple tank top that brightened her eyes to a shade of emerald.

"Come in. I have the beast in lockdown at the moment."

He brushed by her and a whiff of her scent clung to him. He clenched his hands tighter around the reusable totes. "Where to?"

"Straight back is the kitchen."

Kat's kitchen was small but efficient. A nice movable

island for prep work stood in the center and her appliances seemed to be up to date.

"I didn't know what you might need," she said. "Hopefully I have everything."

"I went pretty basic with the menu, just in case."

"Geez, all I get is basic?"

"Sometimes simple is perfect." He stared at her.

Kat smiled and ducked her head. "That is so true."

Every time she blushed her skin took on the loveliest shade of peach. Her freckles popped, and he wanted to explore each one. He also wanted to know if the blush extended to other places. A thought not conducive to food preparation or loose-fitting khaki pants.

"What can I do?" she asked.

"Preheat the oven to 375. And I need a pot for pasta."

When her back was turned, he dropped the bags onto the island and faced the sink, adjusting his pants and counting to ten, thinking of the ice baths he took after every practice. Satisfied a tent wasn't going to appear any longer, he turned back to find Kat staring at him.

"You okay?"

"Great," he said. "Now, how involved do you want to be?"

Her eyes bugged, and he took a deep breath. "With dinner and preparing it."

She smiled. "About as involved as pouring a glass of wine and watching you work."

"Okay then. Pour me a glass too, if you don't mind, and I'll show you my skills."

They settled into a rhythm, Trent dicing, slicing, and sautéing as Kat asked questions and occasionally fetched something he needed.

Riley ventured in once, and Trent tossed him a piece of cheese.

"Um, you might have just made a friend for life," Kat said and shooed the dog back out of the kitchen.

He popped a loaf of garlic bread into the oven and wiped his hands on the dishcloth tucked in the waist of his pants. "No problem with that. I'll be happy to keep your dog in cheese."

"Will you?"

Her voice dropped three octaves and nailed him right in the chest. He froze as she set her wine glass down and crossed the small space to him. "In case I forget."

She rose onto her tiptoes and kissed him. A simple brush of her lips against his. Her hand scorching his cheek and leaving him branded. "Thank you."

She lowered her feet but kept her hand at his cheek. He covered it with his own. "It is my pleasure."

Had they crossed out of research territory, or rather crossed into research of a different nature? How did one even suggest that maybe what should have been a simple meal had turned into a date? A date he wanted to repeat over and over.

Trent opened his mouth to ask even one of the questions, but she stepped away from him and put space between them.

"So, where did you learn to cook?"

He laughed and circled the small island. "Better question might be why did I learn to cook?"

She took a sip of wine. "Okay, why?"

"Tasha."

Kat choked.

"I see you can make the connection."

"Is she always that bad?"

"Yes, and I love her anyway. As do Pete and Tilly."

"That does seem like true love. Maybe he should buy her cooking lessons."

Trent dumped a few olives in the salads. "He has. Several times."

"Oh dear."

"That's a good tip for your research, right? Love someone despite their flaws."

When she didn't answer, Trent looked up to see Kat tracing the rim of her wineglass. "Kat?"

"Some flaws are not possible to overcome."

He crossed over to her and tucked a piece of hair behind her ear. "Speaking from experience?"

She nodded to the countertop. He placed a finger under her chin and forced it up to meet his gaze. "I can't imagine any flaw you possess being impossible to overcome." He kissed the tip of her nose. "Except maybe your grammar."

She shoved him in the chest and laughed. "Seriously, let it go."

The oven timer went off and Trent pulled the bread out. "Ready to taste just how perfect simple can be?"

Chapter 7

"WE HAVE A PROBLEM."

Oh boy, did they. Not only had a simple dinner brought many complex emotions to the surface, but then the damn man had offered to bake dessert. Oatmeal-raisin cookies, her favorite.

She wiped the remaining flour from the counter, weighing any and all responses. "What?" Short and concise. Unlike anything she was feeling regarding the man who'd asked the question.

"Snow."

Kat threw the towel into the laundry room and crossed to the living room window. "Flurries are common. Surely you haven't been gone so long from Decker Springs to not — Holy crap! How long were we in the kitchen?"

She could barely make out either vehicle through the white blanket. It was almost impossible to see individual flakes. Massive tufts swirled this way and that.

A gust of wind rattled the panes, and Riley whimpered and bolted for the pile of blankets on the couch.

"I might be able to make it?"

The question on what should have been a statement gave her pause. He *might* make it, but he might not. Then again, the last thing her mixed-up emotions needed was close proximity to Trent, with a cozy fire to warm them and a blizzard blasting outside. But his safety was more important than any confusion her brain seemed to have.

"You might?"

How Trent would have answered, she didn't find out. Another gust blasted the house, and the lights flickered and died.

"Noooo."

Trent laughed. "Bit dramatic for a woman who lives on the top of a mountain. This can't be your first outage up here."

"A woman who's lived on a mountain for a little over two months, and who has a limited supply of firewood."

He motioned to her living room. "You've got books."

The sound of her mouth falling open echoed in the small house. Even Riley growled from under his blanket fort.

"I believe you said you were leaving."

He laughed and shook his head. Grabbing her by the shoulders, he turned her toward the kitchen. "I was kidding, and there's no way I'm leaving you here to become Mrs. Olaf."

"Aww, you've seen *Frozen*? I love that little guy…"

Trent's face was a combination of concern and amusement.

She swallowed hard and kept moving. "Clearly not the point you were trying to make."

"Clearly." He looked around and back to her. "What's the smallest room in the house?"

"The bathroom."

He held up two fingers about an inch apart. "Little bigger than that."

She blushed. The warmth spread up her throat and across her cheeks. Good grief, it wasn't like she was about to proposition him. "My bedroom."

His hands dropped. "And I suppose it has a fireplace?"

She nodded.

He turned away and mumbled, "Figures."

She gathered blankets and provisions and Riley while Trent ferried loads of wood up to her tiny room.

"You know you really don't have to—"

Brown eyes speared her with intent, and she swallowed the rest of her words. It was a self-perseveration attempt. Here this amazing, almost-too-good-to-be-true man was single-handedly making sure she wouldn't become a popsicle. How on earth could a girl not imagine the best way to stay warm with someone like him in a tiny room with a bed.

It's his fault for being such a damn good kisser. And cook. And family man. And...

True, but it was also just pure lust and a lot of attractive qualities combined with a woman who liked sex and hadn't had any in a while.

No sex. Just heat.

She snorted, and Trent looked over his shoulder from a spot in front of the fireplace.

"Something funny?"

"Nope. Nothing at all." She needed to remember that thought. It would work perfectly in her book.

The other problem with her tiny room was there was nowhere to sit but the bed. And the bed was only a queen. Not so bad if it was just her, but add in a six-foot-three linebacker and that didn't leave a lot of breathing room, or oxygen. Body heat, though, was doing a nice job of warming the room, along with the small fire Trent had coaxed.

"So, don't suppose you have a deck of cards?" He stood and moved to the other side of the bed.

"No, sorry. I do have a puzzle, although a bed isn't the best place to work on one."

Trent lay back and shook his head. "Yeah, beds tend to be best for two things."

Kat stared, unbelieving that he went there.

"What? You were thinking it too. I mean, we are adults who like each other."

She continued to stare.

"We do like each other, don't we?"

"Define like?"

The throw pillow he'd moved to the floor suddenly bounced off her head.

"Sure, that's a great way to induce a female to like you." She launched it back at him, but he caught hold of her wrist and pulled her toward him. She went willingly, until she lay partially on top of him.

"What does induce Kat Evans to like a man?" His voice had dropped several octaves and goosebumps erupted across her flesh as heat burned low in her belly.

The pillow dropped to the floor, and she adjusted her position to bring their faces more even. "Honesty, integrity, trust."

Trent ran a fingertip over her cheekbone. "Things you haven't always had from men in the past?"

She shook her head.

"You deserve every one of those traits and more."

They stared at one another. Kat didn't know what she was looking for, and maybe neither did Trent.

"Can I kiss you?"

She kissed him.

Then she slid further across his body, lying fully on top. He wrapped his arms around her lower back and groaned as she dove deep into his mouth, sweeping her tongue across his. He met her stroke for stroke as his hands ran up and down her spine. His thumbs brushed the sides of her breasts and she arched like a cat, grinding her pelvis into his, providing better access to her sensitive chest.

"I want to touch your skin. Can I, Kat? Can I feel how silky it is?"

"Yes," she breathed and sucked on his lip. His hand slid under the edge of her shirt and the first contact of skin on skin branded her. For as large and solid as Trent was, his movements were that of someone exploring a priceless artifact. Each touch gentle and reverent.

Deeming it fair play, she sat up and slid back till she straddled an area that was all too happy to have her warming it. She unbuttoned his shirt and spread it wide, unable to stop from licking her lips.

"Wow."

He chuckled. "Stop, you're making me blush."

"Oh, don't worry. It won't be the last time." She traced the ridges with her tongue. Trent gasped and shifted with each sweep, muscles bunching under her delicate scrutiny. She licked first one nipple then the other before blowing on them.

"God, Kat." He pushed up into her pelvis.

"Down, boy."

"I need to see you. Please?"

She flicked a nipple and smiled. Reaching for the hem, she lifted her shirt up and over her head.

"Sweet Jesus, am I lucky."

"Maybe you should show some gratitude?" She unhooked her bra and let it slide down her arms.

"All. Night. Long. I promise."

She didn't have a response as Trent sat up and flipped them over, setting his lips to her nipple and proceeding to make love to it. Her breasts had always been her most sensitive area, and with each suck, nibble, and kiss, she grew hotter and wetter. The urge to drag him closer, to feel him inside her caused her to squirm and moan.

He switched his attention to the other breast while his fingers took over torturing the first.

This was how one stayed warm in a snowstorm.

Determined to not miss all the fun, she slid her hand down and beneath the waistband of his pants. He paused and met her gaze. "May I?" she asked.

"Oh, hell yes," he replied and dove back into his worship of her breasts. He shifted to the side and it allowed her more freedom. The head of his cock was as silky as her favorite pashmina. A drop of liquid found its way out and she wrapped her hand around him and ran it down as far as their position would allow.

Trent paused and groaned, shifting a bit more and allowing her to explore.

"I think we have too many clothes on," she suggested as she ran her hand back up his length and scraped a fingernail gently across his head.

"I totally agree."

Before she could go to work on his pants, he had her flat on her back and was dragging her leggings and panties down her legs.

"Damn you're beautiful. All curves and length and…"

She risked a glance to see him staring at her. Pure lust and fascination etched in his granite face.

He closed his eyes and shook his head. "So. Very. Lucky." He opened them back up and smiled at her. "Thank you for trusting me."

Warmth of a totally different kind spread throughout

her. Care. Consideration. Acceptance. Sex was a whole new playing field with that thrown in the mix.

"Your—"

Her instructions were lost on a groan. Trent had dropped between her legs and now explored her with an intensity she didn't know a man could have. He kissed and licked up one side of her and down the other, then used his fingers to part her. His first taste brought her up off the bed, and when his fingers shifted up a bit and exposed her clit, she couldn't help but beg. "Please."

He took his time. A nibble here. A lick there. When he finally covered her with his mouth, his lips sucking her in, she exploded in a rush of orgasmic pleasure. As she arched off the bed again, he continued to work her until the last pulses rang out. He hadn't even penetrated her, and it had been one of the most powerful orgasms she'd ever experienced.

Trent dropped kisses onto her inner thigh and ran his hand along her leg, stretching and extending it while he ran his fingers up and down her skin.

"Do I get in on this action?" she asked.

He grinned. "What if I'm selfish and want to lavish everything on you, no return necessary?"

Kat slid up the bed slightly out of his reach. "I like give and take. The more I give, the more you can take." She pointed to his pants. "Now strip."

Trent crawled off the bed and dropped his pants to the floor, leaving him clothed in tight boxers. Every inch of him dipped and swayed, and one area jutted for attention.

"I can take care of that, you know."

"I have no doubt of your capabilities. I'm just not sure I can handle it."

Kat rose up onto her knees, and Trent's gaze dropped to take in her naked form. "A big, tough, football player like you is going to be done in by a little redhead like me?"

Trent slid his thumbs into the waistband of his boxers. "There's nothing little about you, Kat. You're strong and fierce, and a force that has busted into my orbit and wreaked havoc with my equilibrium."

He slid his boxers down, and she couldn't help but stare. She'd seen a pretty good depiction of Trent Hawkins naked from his magazine spread, but the juicy part had been strategically hidden.

Thank god, because had she seen it, she probably would not have embarked on this take-charge attitude. But she backed up her words and crooked her little finger.

He stalked the small space to her and devoured her mouth in a kiss so hot she almost ripped a condom out of the little basket on her nightstand and ordered him to take her right there.

But she wasn't done taking charge.

"Lie back and think of England."

He lay back and she started to slide down his body. He stopped her with a finger under chin. "You. I can only think of you."

Unable to process any hidden meaning, she slid the last few inches and took him into her mouth.

Trent gripped the quilt on the bed and wished to god he'd listened to instincts to not let this force of nature take charge. Her mouth was delivering all sorts of wicked goodness to his cock and the blood had left his brain so long ago he wasn't even sure he was still breathing. Her hair fell in waves, having come loose during her rather powerful orgasm, and now it acted as a veil, leaving the siren behind it to deliver passionate torture the likes of which he could have only dreamed. With every sweep of her tongue he grew harder, the pressure building to an unimaginable conclusion.

"Kat…" Lord, she was living up to her word. "Kat."

"Hmm." She looked up and licked her lips.

"I'm not going to presume that this"—he waved his hand around—"is leading to the final act, but." He paused and closed his eyes as Kat ran her fingers up and down his length, making it even more difficult to complete his thought. "If you would like to have a final act, then you need to stop. Now."

She laughed, the sound melodic and cooling him slightly as his heart warmed. She laid her head against his thigh. "Would you be disappointed if there were no final act?"

"Of course not. You could walk away now, and while I would be in severe pain and need to use your bathroom for a few minutes, I would respect your decision." He closed his eyes again. "But there's no promise that I won't imagine what the final act would have been like. Everything I have seen and experienced with you is perfect for my imagination."

A rush of cool air spread over him, and he opened his eyes to see her walking around the room. Well, it looked like a hand job was in his future. Either that or a really cold shower.

"If I hadn't already had a clear plan in mind, that little speech of yours sealed the deal." She reached into a basket and held up a foil wrapped package. "Can I do the honors?"

"God, yes."

She crawled up on the other side and ripped the foil with her teeth. After fully suiting his cock up, she ran her fingers up his chest and kissed him. "I like being on the bottom."

The execution of the flip was something worthy of putting in her book. She wrapped her legs around him and the tip of his cock settled at her inviting entrance. Their gazes met and held as he slid in inch by inch. Suddenly, going slow seemed perfect for them. She shifted and spread to accommodate him, and there was nothing more powerful than watching her watch him with trust and concern as her body accepted his. Once fully seated, he smiled. "You okay?"

She leaned up and kissed him. "Show me what you got, big boy."

It was a sultry challenge, one he was gladly accepting. He withdrew almost completely then slid back in, and her eyes closed on a sigh. The little moans and breaths came quicker as he picked up his pace. Kat shifted and gripped him tighter, allowing him closer. She arched on the next thrust with a cry, her nails digging into his back. He was so close, but he would be dammed if he went before her.

Another thrust and he slid an arm under her back, arching her to him. The next thrust and he took a nipple in his mouth and sucked. She tightened her wetness around him and he thrust again, this time nibbling at her sensitive skin. Together, her arching and meeting him thrust for thrust, they climbed toward completion. One final impact and she clenched tight around him, screaming as her muscles pumped him, until his groan joined hers. He kissed her abused nipple and lowered her to the bed, tiny waves of pleasure still rippling around his shaft. He tried to shift off her, but she held firm.

"I like your weight on me."

He liked his weight on her, in her. Hell, he liked her. Period. She ran her fingers up and down his spine and he shifted just slightly, so the brunt of his weight rested on his hip and not hers.

They were sweaty and warm, and yet they clung to one another as their breathing returned to normal.

"I'll be back, I promise." He kissed her soundly and disentangled himself. "Bathroom?"

"To the left."

After a quick disposal of the condom and a wipe down, he returned to their little snowstorm bungalow with a wet washcloth. As he shut the door, he turned to find Riley's little snout peeking from his blankets. He looked a bit judgmental, and Trent smiled. Riley burrowed back into his fort.

He handed over the washcloth.

"Thank you."

Kat cleaned herself and hopped up and left. He enjoyed the view, her ass heart-shaped and jiggly and perfect. A view he could stare at from behind if they ever progressed that far.

Once she came back in, they slid beneath the covers and he gathered her up in his arms. She laid her head on his chest and played with his chest hair. Wind howled, ice stinging against the panes of the bedroom window.

"I'm beginning to have a fondness for spring snowstorms."

Kat looked up at him. "They're climbing my favorites list as well."

$$\text{———————————}$$

Chapter 8

$$\text{———————————}$$

TEN DAYS TO DEADLINE

Kat awoke to a red-gold glow filtering through her windows. Trent's chest rose and fell in a steady rhythm under her cheek. She expected panic to fly in and cool the comfortable warmth of the bed. Questions about what she'd been thinking or how she could do something like that. But none materialized. Instead, she listened to Trent's breathing and inhaled the scent of the two of them cocooned in her bed. Away from the world, from the past, from what might be.

She just wanted the now.

"Morning." Trent kissed her temple and tugged her closer, if that was possible.

"Morning." She was totally grateful he hadn't tried for a kiss. Not that she minded kissing him, far from it. But her breath probably could use freshening, and she didn't want to know what his was like in the morning.

"You okay?"

"I'm great."

He hummed and ran his hand down her back. "So am I."

They lay in silence, Kat tracing circles on his chest.

"I hesitate to ask this and ruin the moment, but… ummm…is this research going to end up public?"

She pushed up to look him in the face, breath be damned. "What do you think?"

He searched her face. "Well, I thought it was pretty damn spectacular from my point of view, and while I have no problem with the emotions being conveyed, I'd rather the details stay private." He smiled. "And I think you would too. You strike me as someone who values her privacy."

Warmth of a completely different kind infused Kat. How had he picked up on that? He'd looked at her and seen past the surface, found an important part of her makeup. He was right. She would never share the details of this. Even anonymously in one of her books.

She lay back down. "Emotions, definitely."

"Kat?"

"Hmmm."

"Why do you value your privacy so much? How did you end up here?"

And in that moment, in the confines of her mountaintop bedroom surrounded by snow and warmth and safety, she told him. She confided about her almost-marriage to the two-faced trust fund baby. How she'd been accused of riding his coattails, and how when she'd left him at the altar, the press had a field day blaming her for all sorts of things.

"The week leading up to the wedding was the worst. Every time he interreacted with anyone he deemed beneath him, he was demanding and cocky—things he hadn't been when it was just the two of us. And I kept telling myself it was the stress of the wedding, but when he got a waiter fired at our private wedding-morning breakfast because there were four sprigs of parsley instead three, and followed that up with a comment about the amount of food on my plate and my ability to fit in my wedding dress, well… I knew I had been living in a fantasy rather than facing reality. I had convinced myself that the man Chad showed the world was fake and the man he showed me in private was real. I was wrong."

With each sordid detail of her past, the chest under her cheek grew harder. The arms surrounding her grew as taut as a rubber band about to snap. The soothing motions on her back slowed then stopped, and regret replaced the trust and safety she'd felt a moment ago. Why had she thought the afterglow the best night of sex she'd ever had would be the perfect time to unload her baggage?

She moved to pull away, but he held her close. "Don't suppose he plays football or does a charity thing I could sign up for and let him know just how much of a bastard I think he is?"

It was her turn to stiffen. "What?" she croaked.

"He sounds like a stuck-up asshole, and you sound like a woman who's been through a PR fire and lived to tell about it. It sucks, and I'm so sorry you had to go through it. And in such an undeserving way. Finding out someone you thought you could love and trust is unworthy hurts worse than losing that person, I think."

How could she respond to that? To something that hit the nail on the head so perfectly it was as if she was confessing to a diary?

"You deserve better, Kat."

"Thank you."

Trent took a deep breath, and Kat prepared herself.

"How did you find the strength? I mean to move past

the fear. Or maybe you weren't afraid." He laughed. "Who am I kidding? I've seen you in action. You're fearless."

She laughed. "I was afraid, Trent. Very. And I had a lot of unwanted input from my family. I'm still not sure some days I will make it. I mean, I didn't have enough wood for a freak snowstorm. You could have showed up here tomorrow to find a popsicle."

He hugged her. "You would have figured it out."

She smiled. There had been something in his tone. A question in the question.

"What do *you* fear?"

She whispered it, afraid maybe it was too personal. They were lying naked in each other's arms, so it didn't get much more *physically* personal than that. But this was soul-deep personal. And she would totally understand if he didn't feel the same trust in sharing.

"Life after football."

She sat up. "What?"

His gaze dropped to her exposed chest and she tugged the quilt to cover herself.

He sighed and slid up in the bed. "What am I without pro linebacker attached to my name? Who is Trent Hawkins? The answers to those questions are what keep me up at night. Keep me from fully deciding whether to retire or not."

"You want to retire?" She didn't know much about football, but usually men seemed to be forced out because of age or they got hurt. And Trent hadn't even reached thirty yet. "Are you hurt?"

"Did I seem hurt last night?"

She refused to blush and stared, waiting for his answer.

"No, I'm not hurt," he said. "My contract is up, and I've been trying to decide if I should leave now and go out on my own terms rather than be forced out by an injury or the inability to compete at my previous level." He shrugged. "I'm not getting any younger, and the new players are practically babies."

"That's pretty damn courageous."

"It's pretty damn terrifying."

"I can see that too."

He closed his eyes and she noticed the lines in a face that normally was smooth and chiseled. The beginnings of a scruff shadowed his chin and cheeks.

"If you could do anything right this second with guaranteed success, what would it be?" she asked.

"Open a bakery."

His eyes flew open, a look of disbelief on his face. It must have matched the look on hers because he burst into laughter. "You should see yourself right now."

She bounced up and down, and once again Trent's eyes darkened. "Stop that right now or this talk is going to be over, and I'm going to show you just how healthy I am."

She scooted away from him and settled. "Sorry, it's just…that's fabulous. You want to bake. Why don't you?"

Now he looked at her like she'd lost one too many marbles. "Cause I could fail. Cause the headlines would mock me for years. Cause I could ruin a good thing."

"Or you could succeed, like you apparently always have. You could create something that is you. You could discover that the true Trent Hawkins is a genius with flour and sugar."

Trent grabbed her and kissed her to within an inch of her life. It seemed morning breath didn't matter after all, because she found herself kissing him right back. He slid on top of her, and the weight of him sent delicious warmth and anticipation licking across her skin.

He stopped and met her gaze. "Thank you for believing. For laughing with me and not at me."

She traced his cheek. "Fear is powerful. I know that more than anyone. But hope and trust can knock it down a peg or two. I have both in you."

"You. Are. Amazing."

He then proceeded to show her just how amazing *he* could be.

$$\overline{}$$

Chapter 9

Eight Days to Deadline

When Kat had suggested two weeks of research, she'd thought she might follow Trent around a handful of times, catalog why women swooned at his feet, and then she would incorporate said swooniness into her book.

She hadn't counted on being one of the swoonees, or rather *the* swoonee. Her research had transitioned from her being an outside observer to being the recipient of all of Trent's moves. Only they weren't moves. They were inherently Trent. Here in Decker Springs he was just Trent Hawkins, hometown boy. And she was currently working on being his hometown girl by all appearances.

And that no longer scared her as it had the night they'd had dinner at Tasha's.

Since the night of the snowstorm, they had spent at least a handful of hours together every day...and the nights. The hero in her book had taken on a lot of admirable qualities, but had also developed a vulnerability. She sensed that same vulnerability in Trent. When a resident would ask about the upcoming season, his answers seemed assured if not obscure, but Kat could see the uncertainty and fear in his eyes and even in his movements following the interactions. For a person who seemed to like control and had the reins of his future in his hands, he certainly was shying away from giving those horses their head.

"You should start a book club."

Kat looked up from her laptop. Trent sat in the armchair, Riley draped across his lap. He'd been talking to his agent earlier and now worked a crossword puzzle with one hand while providing world-class belly rubs with the other.

"A book club?"

He looked at her. "Yeah, at the local library. They would love it, and it would get you in front of some more readers."

"Can I serve something from your bakery?"

His smile faltered. "I haven't made up my mind, Kat. I promise I'll tell you when I do."

"Fair enough. Definitely a good idea. Although, if I don't manage to get this book right and turn it in on time, I may not have to find any readers."

"Am I not providing enough research material?"

He dropped his crossword onto the floor and shifted Riley off his lap, much to her dog's dismay.

She stared, mesmerized, as he prowled over to her and caged her in on the couch. She licked her lips in anticipation and Trent did not disappoint. He gently removed her laptop and set it on the floor, then he dropped to his knees and took her mouth in a brutal kiss that curled her toes and even had Riley growling low.

"You're making him jealous," she said.

"Well, if that makes him jealous, what will this do?"

He scooped her into his arms and carried up to the

bedroom, depositing her on the bed and covering her with his body, just the way she liked it.

"How about a little refresher in this department, and then maybe we can add some new details to this aspect of your research?"

"Hmmm, you know how I love details."

Chapter 10

Trent had helped plan and execute some of the most flawless plays on a football field, but whatever he was doing now would have ended up on the blooper reel. He would blame it on the post-sex glow, but truthfully, it was pure selfishness mixed with a haze of desire. Asking Kat to attend this function knowing how she felt about her privacy, knowing her past…

What have I done?

He tugged his tuxedo sleeves taut and adjusted the cuff links. Despite the tux having been custom made to fit his nontraditional dimensions, it seemed claustrophobic and tight, like one wrong move and the seams would burst. Kat's hotel door loomed three feet away, and all he had to do was knock. They had been expected downstairs about five minutes ago, and yet he couldn't make a fist and raise his hand. Why had he insisted she come? Why had he thought to put her through this gamut of fakeness?

Because there's no one else I would want by my side, and no one I ever have.

The truth was there, but that was what made the unease in the back of his throat even thicker. He didn't want her to see him this way. He didn't want her exposed to the sharks circling down there. And yet she was his life-line right now. The one good anchor in a world about to be even more topsy-turvy than it already was.

This was ridiculous. He'd stared down the front line of some of the toughest pro football teams. Surely one evening at a charity function with a girl he adored was doable.

He stepped up and knocked before the internal arguments could begin again.

The door opened immediately, and Trent's throat swelled for a whole different reason. Kat stood before him, a vision in emerald green. The top of her dress—panels of swirling lace—met a shiny satin skirt that fell in waves to her feet. Her auburn hair was pulled to the side and clipped with a rose-gold comb. He already knew she was worth more than any gem, but seeing her now brought home just how precious she was.

He swallowed three times before he managed a very breathless, "You look stunning."

Kat ducked her head and pink slid across the bridge of her nose. "Thank you."

Trent stepped into her room and wrapped his arms around her waist. She looked up and smiled. "No, I mean it. You are stunning, and not just because of how you look tonight."

He brushed his lips against hers, and she melted into his embrace. Part of him—the selfish part that wanted to listen to all of his worries—urged him to keep kissing her and spend the next hour peeling the dress from her inch by inch, exploring the skin beneath.

The business part knew that if he didn't show up, all

sorts of sordid stories would be headlining tomorrow morning's news. If he decided to leave professional football, he wanted to control it, do it on his terms.

And that meant attending this god-awful shindig.

He deepened the kiss for ten more seconds then pulled back. "I could do that all night."

"Why don't you?" She slid her hand up underneath his hair, which he'd left down for the occasion, and scraped a nail down his neck.

He yanked her closer. "I have to go down there. The vultures will be circling otherwise."

She sighed. "I figured you'd say that." Pulling away, she crossed to the bed and swiped up a beaded clutch.

"Let's get this show on the road."

She smiled, but Trent saw through it. Her eyes lacked the sparkle her genuine smiles always produced. The unease from the hallway returned full force, like a hit in the back from an unfriendly tackle.

Kat snagged a glass of champagne off a passing tray and downed half in one gulp. She wasn't going to get drunk, but surviving this melee called for more than tepid Perrier. She should have fought harder upstairs to keep Trent and his lips occupied, but deep down—once she waded through the impending doom lining her stomach—she knew he always held to his obligations, and this was for a good cause. The Phoenix Legacy fought tirelessly against pediatric cancer, and Trent Hawkins had been the largest donor for the past three years. Not showing up would have been a snub to the charity.

A familiar arm slid around her waist. "Sorry about that. I needed to speak to my agent for a moment."

"No worries." She took another sip to chase the lie down her throat.

She felt his gaze and knew he saw the strain she was working hard to hide. "How about we dance?"

She set the glass down and smiled. "I would like that."

They had taken two steps when a brunette in four-inch heels cut them off. "Trent, dear, I was beginning to think you wouldn't show."

Only because her arm was looped through his, something the woman made note of, did Kat feel the change in Trent's body.

"I haven't missed this event in five years." His curt tone sliced between the space.

"Well, I thought maybe this year, with you retiring…?" She batted thick lashes above beautiful brown eyes at him. She was good. Kat knew Trent hadn't made his decision yet. At least, she didn't think he had, since he hadn't shared and had promised he would.

"That decision hasn't been made." He released Kat and crossed his arms. "When it has, darling, you'll be the first to know."

The schmoozy voice Trent employed slid along Kat's skin, and she had to force herself not to step away from him. *It's just a show.*

They left the brunette pouty but with a definite gleam in her eye.

"Will you really give her the scoop?"

Trent shrugged. "Maybe? Her or Adara. Women working in sports reporting, despite making strides, still get the shit end of the stick. They produce some of the best material out there and are still overlooked. If I can help in any way, I try."

There's the man I know.

"I'm sorry about not introducing you. I thought you

might want to keep yourself as private as possible, but I will if you want me to. I'm proud to have you on my arm." He kissed her fingers. "Totally your call."

"Being mysterious has its perks."

"Mysterious it is."

He slid his arm around her, and they made it five steps this time before a burly gray-haired man stopped them. "What's this shit I hear about you retiring? Man, you got seasons left. Make them force you like I did."

Trent shook the man's hand and clapped him on the back. "No decision yet." He stroked his chin. "Would be nice to collect a few more million."

The gray-haired man laughed, and they moved on. Again, Trent's tone and actions rubbed Kat the wrong way.

"Money factoring into your decision?"

He stopped and turned to her, no doubt a reaction to the unintended sharpness in her voice. "Of course not."

She cut her eyes back to the burly man in retreat.

"That's just playing the game with him. The last thing I need is for him to even think he knows what I am going to do. I learned early on you play to the player if you want to keep your head straight and your morals intact."

"Morals?"

"Kat, what is wrong?"

What *was* wrong? She was here with a man who made her knees weak and her kitchen a disaster. He was even protecting her identity. And yet with every interaction, the fake Trent Hawkins was wiping the real Trent Hawkins away. Or maybe she was scared she didn't know the real Trent Hawkins. She'd been down that road before. She knew her judgement was faulty. She had the slightly used wedding dress to prove it.

She glanced up, ready to tell him, but the look of genuine concern in his eyes tempered her unease.

"Nothing. I'm sorry. It's just, you know this isn't my scene."

He kissed her nose. "I know, and I'm very thankful you're here with me, knowing how hard it is for you."

With that, Trent led them to the dance floor, ensuring no one else waylaid them.

Dancing eased some of her concerns, with Trent whispering in her ear, alternating between suggestions for after the event and new recipes he wanted to try, when the suggestions got too overheated for them both.

Two songs later and most of Kat's worries had fled the room. In front of her was the man she'd seen the night of the snowstorm. The man who baked her cookies and rubbed her dog's belly. The man who played catch with his niece and waltzed with her in the backyard. The man she thought was worth risking her heart.

"Hawkins!"

They both turned to see a slim, dressed-to-the-nines, chiseled-jawed man eating up the floor between them, a camera hot on his heels. "I see you have a lovely date, as always." The microphone was shoved into Trent's face as a bright light lit up both he and Kat. She slid away, and Trent thankfully let her go.

"I'm thrilled to hear the event is once again surpassing expectations," Trent said. "Tonight's festivities are benefiting children all over the country."

Kat was torn between relief that Trent had changed the subject and anger that he hadn't stood up and said she wasn't just another piece of arm candy.

"Ahh, I guess the lovely redhead is off limits. No worries, my people are good."

Kat squeezed her fist and calculated the best way to

mess up Mr. Square Jaw's perfect angles. She hadn't grown up with three brothers without learning a thing or two.

"Do you have something meaningful to ask, Dick, or are you just slinking through, picking up what the honest reporters are dumping?"

"I'm asking what every other person in the room is too afraid to ask. We all saw you making lovey eyes on the dance floor. I'm just the one who's going to figure it out. Privacy is non-existent in your world, and you damn well know it."

With that, Dick and his camera disappeared into the crowd. Kat watched him get swallowed up and switched her gaze to Trent to see him pinching the bridge of his nose. She placed a hand on his bent arm and he stepped back. "Will you excuse me for a minute?" he asked.

"Of course."

He left her standing there, half the room glancing at her or the ceiling or the floor, depending on if she was looking at them or not. The nausea climbing up her throat was familiar. This lifestyle, this fakeness, this camera in your face and your life splashed across the screen. It was all familiar. She'd traveled this road, and it ended no place she wanted to go to again. She'd thought she could handle it with Chad, knowing the real person behind the mask. But she'd been wrong. The mask had been for her not for the social whirl. The only question was, how much longer would this be Trent's world, and could she possibly hang on long enough to see it through? And maybe the bigger question was, which Trent was the truth? Did he put his mask on for society or for her?

***

Trent walked Kat to her room but stopped her from

opening the door. "I'm sorry about Dick. He, well, he's a dick. I usually handle him better."

"It's fine."

Trent didn't believe that any more than he believed that nothing had changed. Kat had immediately put up a shield after their run in with the infamous trash reporter. He didn't blame her. Dick had taken his slumming to a whole new level. He had a feeling it was due to the rumors circulating that Dick was on his way out thanks to a whole slew of lawsuits about to be filed over harassment. Still, could Trent have done more to shield Kat?

Yeah, I could have not brought her to begin with.

"Well, I guess I'll see you in the morning."

She picked at the lace on her dress. "About that?"

Shit. "Yes?"

"Could we maybe…" She squared her shoulders and finally met his eyes. "Maybe leave tonight?"

He was so relieved she wasn't completely cutting him off that he instantly agreed. After all, he hadn't initially been planning on spending the night without her, but after what had happened, he didn't think asking himself into her room was the right thing. At least this would allow them some more time together. Captive audience and all that.

"Absolutely. How long do you need?"

She glanced to the door and back to him, and relief etched her peaches-and-cream skin. He hadn't realized how tense she truly was till the strain drained away.

"Twenty minutes."

"Great." He dropped a kiss on her cheek and jogged the few feet to his room. It only took about five minutes to change and get everything into his duffel. Five minutes he spent figuring out the best way through the wall that now stood between them. He was who he was, and tonight was part of that. He knew of her past, but he'd spent more than enough time with Kat for her to see the true Trent, not the dog and pony show he'd put on downstairs. Maybe this wall really was about her aversion to the spotlight and that asshole Dick.

But as they merged onto the highway leading them back to Decker Springs, the silence grew heavier, and the wall seemed reinforced. Every time he opened his mouth to make some joke or ask some question, cotton mouth took over, and he snapped it shut and took a drink of water.

Just after midnight he pulled up to her house, nothing resolved between them.

He hopped out and circled the truck, opening the door. She let him help her down and he thanked the heavens for small favors.

"I can swing by later this morning and take you over to my sister's to get Riley if you like."

She fumbled through her purse and paused. "Sure. Thank you."

He hugged her from behind. "Kat, I am so sorry about this evening. I just wanted you there with me. It was selfish, and I should have thought more about the cost to you."

She spun around in his arms and brushed a kiss across his lips. "I wanted to be there with you too. I'll see you tomorrow."

He let her disappear through the door, but it was only after he was back in his truck heading down the mountain that he realized she hadn't said it was fine. Because they both knew it wasn't.

$$\rule{6cm}{0.4pt}$$

Chapter 11

$$\rule{6cm}{0.4pt}$$

FIVE DAYS TO DEADLINE

"Need some help?"

Kat smiled up at Trent. She wasn't surprised he'd tracked her down after the way they had left things last night, but she'd really hoped that maybe she could get some breathing room before having to face him and his dimples. Although she had no doubt Bella had played a hand in it, since she'd noticed her friend take out her phone and fire off a message not thirty seconds after Kat had settled in at the table.

"Actually, things are moving along. I've sent the first three quarters to my editor to look over while I finish the ending."

"That's…great."

Kat ignored the change in tone. Just as she tried to ignore the effect he had on her. Despite the need to breathe, she was happy he was here, and yet the unease from the charity event had grown exponentially. She hadn't been able to tuck it away as a needless worry.

"So, what are your plans for tonight?"

She grabbed her mug of tea and raised it to her lips. "Just trying to get this in. Basically, being a hermit for the day."

"Oh."

Bella slid a plate in front of Trent. "Let me know if you two need anything else."

Kat closed her eyes and swallowed the lump in her throat. When had they become "you two"? Could they continue to be that even with the two-week deadline coming to an end, and with the eye-opening, gut-wrenching experience from last night?

"I thought I was going to pick you up and grab Riley this morning."

She didn't miss the hurt lacing the statement. How could she explain she needed some space when even she didn't understand it? "I—"

"Trent, Kat, great to see you two."

Kat looked up at the white-haired gentlemen who had approached the table while she was knee-deep in misery. *Good timing.* She had no idea who he was, but clearly he knew her. Or more likely he knew Trent and by association had learned who she was.

Trent stood and shook the man's hand. "Harold, good to see you. How's the theater doing?"

"Good, good. Actually, that's why I'm here bothering you two lovely young people," Mr. Wiggins said. "Trying to organize everyone to get the sets and props done in one day. Kind of a community potluck of work. Didn't know if you two were interested in lending a hand. Won't be for a few days yet."

When Trent didn't answer, Kat risked a glance at him. He looked to her as if to say it was her call. Definitely a testing moment. He was obviously aware of the undercurrents, not to mention the unanswered question lingering across the table.

"Sounds like a fun day of work." Kat smiled at the older gentlemen.

Harold clapped his hands together and beamed. "Wonderful, I'll get the details to you soon."

The man left them, and Kat glanced back to her manuscript.

"You okay?"

She looked at Trent and smiled. "Of course I am. Just trying to meet a deadline and incorporate all the notes I've made," she said, returning her attention to her laptop.

"*All* the notes?"

She darted another glance at him as her face heated. He was grinning, despite the huskiness of his tone. It warmed her and terrified her. How could she continue to battle all these fears, and yet how could she not?

"Every. Single. One."

Trent's eyes darkened, and he rubbed his thumb up and down the coffee mug. She stared transfixed, remembering what those hands and fingers did to her body. What they would do right now if she gave him the right signal.

Loud barks and yips broke though the scene. She glanced behind him out onto the sidewalk to see Tasha and Tilly spinning in circles as Riley and Daisy chased each other.

Kat grabbed her things and hurried out, Trent hot on her heels. "I was going to get him from you when I finished up here. I left a message."

Tasha smiled. "Oh gosh, no worries. After Trent texted you two were here, we thought we would take them to the dog park to get their fidgets out."

Riley beelined for her and nearly knocked her down with his exuberant pawing. Only the wall of heat behind her, who gripped her arms, prevented her from landing on her ass.

"I've got you."

She shouldn't love those words. Shouldn't feel the truth in them. Shouldn't relish in that truth. For how long would he have her? Till their time was up and he went back to playing. Till he realized she wasn't the right piece of arm candy for him. Sure, he'd talked of a future away from professional football, but so far he'd shown no indication he could get past his fear.

She reached for Riley's leash, and she and Tilly worked on getting it untangled. "Thanks, Aunt Kat. I hope it was okay that Riley slept with me last night."

Kat opened her mouth several times. She was Aunt Kat? When had that happened? When had everything come together that screamed she and Trent were a couple? Especially when it was looking more and more like they wouldn't be in a few more days.

She ruffled Tilly's hair. "Of course, although I would have warned you that he's a blanket hog."

Tilly crouched down and rubbed Riley's now-exposed belly. "We came to a compromise."

Kat laughed. "Thank you for taking such good care of him."

"Anytime. He's welcome whenever you need to leave town." Tasha said.

She doubted she would be leaving town again anytime soon, but she wasn't planning on sharing that with Mr. Personal Fireplace behind her.

"Well, I'd better get going," she said. "Thank you again."

She turned and smiled at Trent. "Thank you for letting Tasha know. I'll talk to you later."

Trent watched Kat walk away.

"Hey, what did you do to her?"

He turned to his sister. "Nothing."

"Really? I mean, she couldn't get away from us fast enough. What happened at the charity event?"

"Nothing that doesn't normally happen. You've been there."

"Yes, I have. I have also grown up with you in the spotlight. I know what vultures are and how to handle myself. What about Kat?"

"Kat can handle herself."

"Of course she can, but that's on the outside. What about on the inside?"

Trent knew there was a past. Kat had shared enough for him to know the spotlight wasn't for her, and yet she was in a profession that might provide a stage one day. Then again, she could call those shots. His spotlight she couldn't control.

"I think her inside is struggling."

"What are you going to do about it?"

Trent held his hands out in a plea. "I don't know. If she won't tell me what's bothering her, I can't help her."

"You can't or won't?"

Tasha walked away before he could answer. Wasn't the answer the same in some ways?

He went back inside and paid his bill.

"Leaving?"

"Yeah, I have some football stuff to take care of."

Bella smiled. "You made up your mind yet?"

He had, but he wasn't ready to share that with anyone yet.

"Not yet. I promise you'll know when I do."

"Some things shouldn't be that hard."

He looked closer at Bella. "Maybe, but they are just the same."

"Maybe because you're letting fear control more of the outcome than it should."

Right to the heart of the matter. But he'd learned from experience you didn't give women like Bella the power of knowing they were right.

"Definitely something to think about."

He slapped the counter and left.

Three hours later and he'd done the round of phone interviews that were required of him in the off-season. Three days left in his contract. Three days to make the decision. One less than Kat's deadline. A decision he knew the answer to, and yet he'd sidestepped every one of the reporters when they'd asked. Even the email from his coach and the team owner sat unanswered in his inbox.

His phone chirped, and he found a message from his publicist.

Got the copy of two of the interviews. Both look great. You need to RSVP for the wildlife gala.

Crap, he'd forgotten. He'd gone every year, mostly because it was close by, only attended by league people—meaning no reporters—and it benefited the state wildlife fund. It would be a perfect opportunity to show Kat another side to this public life.

No. Another event right now probably wasn't the best course. But an evening with just the two of them would give them the chance to work past the barrier between them. He wanted to give her his undivided attention.

Should he call her or surprise her at home? He decided that after this morning he would be better served with a call. Two rings had Kat answering. Her hesitant hello spoke volumes.

"Hey, sorry to bother you. I promise it's for a good cause."

"You're not." But he could hear her clacking away on the keys.

"First, I want to apologize for the charity event again."

"I've told you it's fine. I knew what could happen. I'm okay."

"Well, I would also like to make it up to you."

The clacking stopped. "You don't need to."

"I want to, Kat. I want to spend an evening with you that doesn't involve reporters."

"Trent," she whispered, and his heart caught. It wasn't said with endearment, more like resignation.

"I would like to just spend an evening with you. Takeout and a movie or dinner and a show. Whatever you would like. Just the two of us."

Silence answered him. His grip on his phone tightened as his mind raced trying to figure out what she was thinking.

"It's a lovely invitation, but I…can't."

"Is it the time? I mean we could do it tomorrow or the next day."

"I can't, Trent. I'm sorry. I've only got a few days and I really need to get the book finished."

"Sure, bye." But he was already staring at the blinking call-ended notice on his phone.

Pressure built in his head and traveled to the back of his throat. She hadn't even given him a chance to offer the details. To tell her how magical he would make it, because she deserved magic after standing by his side last night. No, she'd just tossed the word "can't" at him and hung up.

Can't.

No explanation or suggestion of another time.

No 'maybe when the book is done,' or 'I wish I could.'

Just can't.

Disappointment fueled his movements as he paced through the house. He'd thought he and Kat had been developing into a team. Learning to work together. Believing in one another. Hadn't they talked about that the night of the snowstorm? Shared their fears and let the other help ease their burdens.

She was backing off. That was the only explanation that made any sense. Despite the disaster of the gala, they should have been able to talk through it. She should have been able to lean on him and discuss her concerns.

Clearly Kat didn't want to lean on him. She wasn't interested in being a team. She was interested in a one-woman road trip, with her past dictating her route.

His life was busy. He'd thought he was only open to something casual, something simple while he figured out his football future and beyond. But after getting close to Kat, he realized he wanted a partner. A true partner. One who understood him—where he came from and where he wanted to go. But Kat didn't seem interested in being that partner.

Chapter 12

The doorbell sent Riley into a fit. Despite the chaos of her corgi doing his best wolf impression, she felt relief. If the bell had been rung, that meant it wasn't Trent. She wasn't ready to face the emotions he brought forth.

Luring Riley into his crate with a huge pile of treats, she snapped the lock and hurried to the door, yanking it open.

She nearly shoved it closed again in his face. "What in god's green earth are you doing here?"

An arm shot out holding a printout of an internet story. In the photo, looking rather attractive—though that clearly was not the point—was Kat, arms around Trent as they gazed into one another's eyes on the dance floor.

"Do I need to explain further?"

Kat sighed and motioned her unwanted visitor in. She went to shut the door, then peeked outside. "It's just you, right?"

Her brother Davis flopped into the armchair beside the

fireplace and sighed. "Trust me, I'm enough. Besides, Daniel and Brandon are both busy with their offspring."

Kat laughed as her youngest brother shivered at the thought. She knew he adored their nieces and nephews, but honestly, she agreed with his assessment that he wasn't father material. Maybe one day, but definitely not today.

"So, how long do I have to be polite before I get to ask what the hell you're thinking slumming with a football player?"

"Slumming? I think we look mighty damn fine, and Trent is no one's idea of slumming."

"Kat, seriously. Wasn't that what this crazy-ass move to this not-near-anything-ass town was all about? To maintain your privacy. Get away from the mess of your almost-wedding."

Her brothers were wrong most of the time, but this once she stared at green eyes so similar to hers and collapsed onto the sofa. "I didn't plan on it."

"No one ever does, do they?"

"Hand it over."

"What?"

"The article. I haven't seen it. I might as well know what I'm facing."

"You haven't talked to Trent about it?"

"No. I…"

Davis tossed some papers to her, the internet story on top. She stared at the photo of them and fought the tears welling up. They did look like two people with eyes only for each other. But that was not what the story said. Two sentences in and her heart ached for an entirely different reason. She glanced at the byline only to see that scumbag Dick Logan listed. He'd done it. Found out who she was—and not only that, found out about her past. He accused her of being a femme fatale, riding another rich man's coattails. And he predicted that, once again, she would leave this rich man high and dry.

The papers slipped from her hands and tears plopped onto the topmost article as they rested in her lap. None of it was true, but she knew that truth in reporting rarely mattered these days. The facts were there, just spun in a way that made her out to be some gold digger. Luckily, he hadn't learned that she was also a romance writer. Thankfully, she'd managed to cover those tracks and keep some of her new life private.

At least for now.

A tissue box came flying into her lap and she choked out a thank you while blowing her nose and trying to soak up some of the waterworks.

"I could hook you up with someone to sue him."

Kat shook her head. She didn't want the media circus of that. Besides, it would all fade and something new would take its place.

"You know there's another article?"

"Thank you, but I've had enough of how horrible a person I am for today."

"It's an interview with Trent."

Kat took a deep breath. She didn't want to read Trent's words. What if they had been twisted, or worse, what if they were truthful and yet not flattering?

"I think you should read it."

She shifted her mountain of tissues to the side and shuffled the pages. There was a single shot of Trent in his tux, a smile on his face as he talked with teammates. This byline was from Adara. As she made her way through the short Q and A, her heart shattered a little more. The final question leaving her both nodding in understanding and holding her breath due to the pain.

What is the hardest thing about being well-known?

Trusting people to see the real me. To recognize who I am without my helmet and pads on. It is next to impossible to play both roles and believe that someone you care for can distinguish.

A bark was the only indication that someone else had arrived. When a light knock sounded, Kat's stomach plummeted worse than the first drop on the four-hundred-foottall roller coaster her older brother Brandon had tricked her onto last summer.

"Do you need me to get that? You look like you did the night of your twenty-first birthday."

Kat shook her head even as the rest of her began to tremble. This article had been the final nail in a coffin she'd already bought. The next five minutes were not going to be pretty.

Chapter 13

Trent paced the small porch, which amounted to about one and a half steps one way, about face, and one and a half steps back. Kat had to be home. Not only was *her* car there but so was some sporty little thing that shouldn't have even made it up the mountain.

Maybe she's with someone?

Gripping the porch railing, he rolled his shoulders. No. She wasn't with someone. Kat wasn't like that. He knew how good and honest she was.

The door opened, and he turned to find her staring with heartbreak in her eyes.

"You saw it didn't you?"

She nodded and stepped out onto the porch closing the door behind her, but not before he caught a glimpse of someone else inside.

"Company?"

Again the nod.

"I'm sorry about this." He held up his phone, a copy of the story on it. "I knew Dick was scum, but this was beyond low even for him. I already have my lawyers on it ready to file if you want them to."

Kat shook her head.

He stepped toward her, and she held her hands out to stop him. "Thank you for checking up on me, but you didn't need to. I'm not your responsibility."

The words, along with the tone, slapped him across the face. "What does that mean?"

"Just that I can handle this if I decide to. But thank you, and thank you for your time over these past days. It's been educational and a tremendous help. My editor loves the changes I've made so far."

"Kat." He didn't recognize the woman in front of him. Despite the rejection yesterday, he'd been thinking on how they could get through this. Once the pain had passed, he'd realized that her past was blocking her road to their future. Of course, this article was a huge boulder in the middle of that road, but he'd moved boulders before.

"Trent, we're kidding ourselves here. I can't be in the spotlight. I came to Decker Springs to get away from it and my past. Being with you brought it right back out into the open. Exposed me to an even bigger spotlight. I'm not arm candy. I can't be the two-faced person you need in your life."

He growled and took another step. "I have never needed nor asked you to be arm candy." He turned away. "Christ, I come here worried out of my mind about you and the impact of this stupid article and you…"

"I'm sorry you're upset, but I have been down this road, and I refuse to travel it again."

"Been down this road? Excuse me. Are you saying there are similarities between me and your ex?"

Kat crossed her arms and dropped her gaze.

"You know, maybe you're right. We shouldn't go down

this road."

Her eyes snapped to his and tears rolled down her face. He couldn't let that get to him now. Right now, he needed the linebacker who was immune to the hits and kept pushing.

"You're letting your past be a roadmap to your future, and it's not going to lead you anywhere you like."

He turned. Two steps and he threw over his shoulder, unable to look at her anymore, "I've shown you the real me. Deep down you know that. And I can believe this is hard for you and not something you wanted." He spun and pointed at her. "But when you go back inside and replay all the time we have spent together, you remember this…" He walked to his truck and opened the door, stepping up onto the running board as he looked across at her one last time, gazing directly into her eyes. "You abandoned me. You lumped me in with your ex, with no proof other than fear and the past, and deemed me not worthy."

Trent climbed in and forced himself not to look back, his chest aching as he tore down the mountain road.

Kat stepped back into her house and was enveloped in a brotherly hug. She let sob after sob wrack her body until Davis steered her upstairs and returned with a hot cup of tea and some cookies.

When she saw the cookies, she burst into a fresh round of tears.

"Jesus, Kat. They're just oatmeal raisin. You didn't have any other kind."

Riley pushed through the door, hopped up onto the bed and crawled into her lap. She ran her hands through his fur and slowed her breathing. They *were* just cookies.

"Feeling better?"

"Not especially, but I did what I had to do, and what was right."

She risked a glance at her baby brother and frowned. "What?"

He held his hands up in surrender. "Nothing. It's your life. You'll travel your own road, as you have told us numerous times."

"That's right. I'm a big girl, and I can handle myself."

Davis got up and headed to the door. "I'll let you rest."

"Thank you. And thank you for being here. I wouldn't have asked you, but I'm glad you're here."

He tapped the door frame and smiled. "Anytime, Sis." He stepped through but paused. "Just one more thing. When you're traveling your road, make sure you're not going in circles."

Left alone, she slid down and burrowed herself in the quilt. Riley circled her feet and curled up next to her.

Despite her brother's words, she knew she'd done the right thing. She may have come to care for Trent, but two weeks was all it could have been. His life was out there, in the papers and on TV, and hers was here on a mountain writing books.

And what if he retires?

That was the question that kept sliding past her defenses and trying to knock her wall of "I did the right thing" down.

Still, it didn't change the article or her past or the fact that Trent Hawkins might always have to play two parts. He didn't have a post-retirement plan. He didn't know anything other than being a famous football player.

You abandoned me.

His words sliced through her skin, and she turned onto her side and stared out the window.

Chapter 14

Trent slid the next pan of brownies into the oven and slammed it shut. Setting the timer, he turned around and leaned against the counter debating what he could whip up next. His phone chirped, and he glanced to see another message from Tasha. Clearing the screen, he circled to the pantry and started digging for butterscotch chips.

The incessant peal of his doorbell had him cursing the whole way to the door.

"Tasha, come in."

She slapped him on the arm as she passed, and he stared out the door debating if he could just leave her here and find someplace else to hide.

"I'll just track you down and then we can have this conversation in public. And I know how much you like juicy stories." She threw her purse on the table.

"Seriously, Tasha. Didn't the twenty-three unanswered messages drop the hint that I want to be left alone?"

Tasha crossed into the kitchen and let out a low whistle.

"No, but the fifty pounds of sugar and flour are getting the message to me loud and clear."

Deciding that letting Tasha say her piece and then leave was the quickest way he could get back to baking, he returned to the pantry. His sister didn't disappoint.

"Have you talked to Kat? She handling this okay?"

"Yes. No. We're done."

Tasha squeezed in beside him in the panty. "What?"

"I talked to her. She was upset about the article. We're over."

"And you're okay with that?"

"Of course. We were pretty doomed from the start anyway. I mean, I really was only around for research purposes."

A bag of rice hit him upside the head, followed by a tug on his ear that led him all the way to his living room.

"Sit."

Trent rubbed the side of his face and sat, crossing his foot over his knee.

"I think you should have an MRI. Maybe you've taken one too many hits, cause the bullshit nonsense coming out of your mouth right now is scaring me.

"Kat made a choice, one I agree with. Case closed."

"You agree that you guys shouldn't be together?"

He nodded, unable to actually voice the lie.

Tasha stomped out of the room and returned with a copy of the article. She shoved the picture under his face— him and Kat dancing. "This is proof that you're both idiots. People kill to have someone look at them like that. I've seen you act—you can't. Are you telling me *Kat* is that good of an actress that you fell for it?"

He pushed by Tasha and went back into the kitchen.

"She doesn't want me. She thinks I'm just like the ex mentioned in the article." He scrubbed his face, which was rough with two days of stubble. "It's like she never even knew me."

Tasha settled on a bar stool. "You don't believe that, Trent, any more than you believe you were just research, or that she doesn't want you."

"It doesn't matter. I need to focus on my decision and deal with the ramifications."

Tasha popped a Russian tea cookie into her mouth. "It does matter, and you damn well know it. Have you made your decision?"

"Yes." And he'd wanted Kat to be the first to know. Kat who had inspired him to take the chance. Whose strength in fighting back against her past was the final bullet on his Pros and Cons list. But she wouldn't be the first—she might not hear about it at all.

———————————————

Chapter 15

———————————————

Two Days to Deadline

Kat circled the block and pulled into an alley. Checking her rearview and finding it empty, she laid her head on the steering wheel and gave a herself a stern talking to. She'd committed to helping the theater. Decker Springs was her full-time home now. Trent was only here a few months of the year. She liked the people, and she wanted to invest more of herself into the town. Which was why she'd agreed to help when Harold had approached them.

Of course, the director probably wanted Trent more than her. Maybe she could just turn around and go home.

But what if Trent didn't show? Then she would be leaving Harold in a bind, and she'd likely be the one having to face his disappointment.

But what if Trent *was* in there?

So what? They'd had their time together, even if shorter than originally planned. She'd done her research and finished her book, turning it in this morning, two days early. No, she'd done what she needed to do.

Then why is my heart a giant ball of pain, and why is the

thought of seeing him filling me with so much hurt that I'm camped out in an alleyway?

No. Dammit, hadn't Trent called her strong? She was strong. Well, she could *be* strong. They were almost the same thing.

Pulling back onto Main Street, she found a parking spot half a block from the theater. Before debate number five could ensue, she grabbed her bag, adjusted her ponytail and jumped out.

"I wasn't sure you would actually do it."

The urge to spin around and squeal shook through her body, but she remained facing away from him.

"I gave my word." And with that, she marched down the sidewalk to the theater.

Thankfully, he didn't follow. At least not right away. She was already through both sets of doors and making her way toward the stage when his presence filtered across her skin. Memories of their snowy night rushed through her, quickly followed by the smiles and confessions afterward. Hot on the heels of those memories was the charity event, then an image of the article.

She slid into one of the rows and collapsed in a seat. This shouldn't be so hard.

"Thank you, everyone, for coming," Harold began. "I believe with all your help we will get this knocked out today."

Whispers and scattered applause echoed off the ceiling.

"Now, I have broken you up into pairs with specific duties for each couple."

Icy dread washed over Kat. She knew without a shadow of a doubt that Trent and she were paired up. She gripped the edge of her seat, intent on pushing up and walking out, when the director hurried over to her. His gaze went behind her.

"You two are on paint duty."

"Mr. Wiggins?"

The director slid a smile her way. He reminded her of Santa Claus, with red rosy cheeks and tufts of snow-white hair sticking in every direction. Was she really going to let Santa Claus down because she was too cowardly to face a man?

"Yes?"

Kat took a deep breath. "Do you happen to have any aprons?"

A small chuckle reached her, and she ignored the rush of warmth crawling up her exposed neck.

"Of course, of course. Why don't you two follow me, and I can get you squared away?"

Kat stood, and sidestepped her way to the aisle. She could feel Trent's heat close behind, not because he'd invaded her space, but because her body just knew he was close enough to touch. To see. What would she see when she finally got the courage to meet his eyes? Would he be able to see how much she was second guessing her decision? How hard this was?

Mr. Wiggins got them settled in the back of the stage, large white screens waiting for their brush strokes laid out across saw horses.

"Now, the show's going to rehearse. I hope you don't mind the distraction."

Yes! She was getting a break. If the show was rehearsing that meant there wouldn't be silence she had to fill. Finally risking a glance at the mountain of a man two feet from her, she sucked in a breath. Hunger and hurt filled his chocolate gaze. She searched his face and noted the tight lines and slightly dark circles under his eyes.

"Not sleeping well?" Crud, why had she invited a conversation?

Trent ran a hand down the back of his neck. "No. I have a lot on my mind."

"Oh." She broke eye contact and went back to stirring the bright-blue paint. Of course he did. She hadn't seen any evidence of his final decision regarding retirement. That kind of life-changing choice would keep anyone up at night.

But a small part of her hoped maybe *she* was keeping him up at night too.

That part was a selfish bitch. She'd broken it off. She thought she'd done the right thing. She was protecting herself even if it hurt him. And really, protecting him too. Wasn't she?

Yep. Selfish bitch.

***

Trent had never worked so hard in his life to block out emotions. It was a skill that was second nature to him on the field, but the past two weeks with Kat had ground that finely-honed skill down to a little nub. He was aware of every breath she took; every slight movement brought a whiff of her scent. And with each monstrous distraction came conflicting emotions. Anger at how easily she'd dismissed him and thrown them away, and desire over how she still heated his blood with her strength and beauty. That strength was on prime display right now. He could see her stilted movements, how much care she took to avoid eye contact. He had no doubt earlier she'd planned to leave, and yet she'd done what he'd seen her do numerous times. She'd straightened her spine and charged full speed ahead.

But he couldn't help asking himself why she felt she needed that strength. Their parting was her doing. She'd made it clear that being with him wasn't part of her plan for the future. If that was her decision, she should have no problem being in the same room with him.

Unless…

She wasn't as confident of her reasons as she thought.

He certainly wasn't. Even now, despite how hurt he was, a small part of him could see things from her side. Could see the similarities and understand her retreat as self-preservation.

It was killing him. He needed to know.

He'd avoided touching her up to this point, but now he reached in front of her for a paint stirrer. She jumped back, paint splattering on the front of her apron and on her face.

"I'm so sorry. Here let me." He swiped up a rag and dabbed at the spot on her cheek. She held her breath and stared at his forearm. The dabbing became wiping, and then he stopped and cupped her cheek.

Her gaze rose slowly, and when her eyes met his, a small part of him swelled with hope.

He dropped his hand. "I think I got it all."

"Thank you."

She shifted around to the other side of the screen, and he let her go. They worked from opposite ends as the cast settled in for another song. He noticed most of the members sitting around the outside and realized just the main male and female characters were together. The posters outside the theater promoted *Newsies*, but he wasn't familiar with the show.

Opening strains rose in a crescendo, and the female launched into a beautiful melody, singing of believing in something, even if for one night.

Trent paused and let the notes and lyrics flow through him. He glanced to Kat to see her brush suspended over the screen, her eyes fixated on the couple now singing to one another.

They pledged that the night was theirs even if tomorrow was uncertain and that having something to believe in gave them hope.

She shifted her gaze to his and they stared at one another as the couple on stage pledged their love to one another. Was it that easy? Believing in one another. Trusting in one another. It should be. He believed in Kat Evans. He believed in what they could be. He loved her.

The song finished to a round of applause, but Kat still stared. He opened his mouth to ask why they were doing this to one another. But before a breath crossed his lips, she dropped her paintbrush and rushed from the stage.

He shoved his brush into the can and moved to follow but froze after two steps. Clearly, she'd had a revelation or a reaction. Neither was going to be fleshed out in her mind, hence the fleeing. Hell, he was still a little unbalanced at discovering he loved her, although he shouldn't be. He'd been under her spell since the first missed comma. But he realized going to her now wasn't going to help either of them. Plus, he had a plane to catch and an announcement to make. No, he needed a plan. He needed a declaration. He needed help.

And he knew just the person to ask.

Chapter 16

Kat's phone chirped, and she swiped to see a Google alert. Closing her eyes, she took a deep breath and tried to imagine which might hurt more: seeing her name once again linked with Trent's or seeing his name linked with someone else's. She rolled her shoulders and nodded. She was a grown-ass adult and she could handle this.

Hawkins going out on top.

Tears pricked her eyes. He'd retired. Was giving up his first love—football. Taking the chance that there was something just as wonderful and fulfilling in his future.

And that's not me.

Wiping her cheeks, she scanned the article to see that he'd made the announcement in Houston yesterday. That meant, for today anyway, that Decker Springs should be safe. At least from him. She could handle the looks and the whispers. She couldn't handle the sight of him.

Thirty minutes later, she found a parking spot a block away from Beans and Leaves. She reached for her satchel, but it tugged back. Yanking, she freed it along with something shiny that flung up to her ceiling and clattered back to the center console. It was the gold medal Trent had given her the day at the elementary school.

She traced the medallion, the metal cool to the touch, and swallowed hard. Would she ever be free of the memories? Did she really want to be? Shaking off the pain, she placed the medal in a cup holder and got out of her car. She kept her head down, avoiding eye contact with the few townspeople out and about. Not the bravest of moves on her part, but everything was so raw, simmering right on the top of her skin, that one shared glance full of pity and she would be a puddle in the middle of Elm Street.

Kat managed to get to the door of Beans and Leaves without tripping or succumbing to the pressure in her eyes. What on earth had she been thinking coming to the place where they'd first met? Where a stupid idea had turned into two weeks of memories that had left her a driveling mess. Her hand wrapped around the door handle and froze. She didn't know if she could do this. Be here. Picture his dimples as he corrected her grammar. If she'd done the right thing in letting him go, why the hell did her heart feel like a piece of AstroTurf trampled by cleats? Lord, he was so immersed in her life that she was using football references. Emotional pain was what she'd been trying to avoid in breaking it off. She couldn't handle the holes in her heart and soul.

"Um, miss, are you going in or out?"

Kat turned to see an elderly gentleman with a grin and dimples.

"Allow me." She opened the door.

"No, ma'am. What kind of gentleman would I be if I didn't allow ladies first?"

Left with no choice, Kat stepped into the café and moved to the side. It was later than normal, and only a few tables were occupied. She should head to one in the back. Be far away from the comings and goings of the door and out of sight of well-meaning townsfolk. But—as if she had no control over her eyes or her body—she spun to the right, to the table where it had all begun.

A bouquet of dahlias sat in the middle, and in front of the vase was a hand-painted sign.

Reserved forever for Mr. and Mrs. Hawkins

A sob erupted, and she stumbled the few steps to the table.

A commotion behind her sent her nerves into a frenzy. Heat washed down her back, leaving her knees feeling like jelly.

"I promise never to correct your grammar again and to spend every day giving you a reason to smile and swoon. I want to be a worthy hero to your heroine."

His voice brushed her ear, her neck, and yet she couldn't turn around. She was so afraid this was a dream. An illusion her heart and mind had created to keep the pain at bay.

"Kat. Darling. Please look at me. Please tell me I have a chance."

A warm hand intertwined with hers. She turned, her vision blurry from the tears openly coursing down her cheeks.

"Shh, honey, there's no need for tears." He wiped his thumb across her cheek.

"I love you," she blurted out, then closed her eyes and dropped her head to his chest. "I'm sorry. You deserve better from me. The writer. I just…"

Trent kissed the side of her head and pulled her in close. "I have never heard three more perfect words in my life."

She looked up into eyes so bright and sure. "I love you," she said again.

"I love you, too. I love your fierce determination and horrible grammar. I love your fat dog and your lack of baking skills. But most of all, I love that you love me, Trent Hawkins the man, and not the image."

He pulled back and led her to the table—their table. "Kat, honey, I mean it. I want this to be our table every day for the rest of our lives." He dropped down to one knee. "Will you marry me?"

Kat knelt on the floor in front of him. "Yes."

The whole café erupted as Trent slid the ring onto her finger. "So, what would happen now if this was in your book?"

Kat kissed him. Her lips brushing his twice before settling and teasing.

Bella cleared her throat. "If you two could take a break, I have something for you."

Kat's cheeks heated, and she smiled as she saw the passion and frustration pumping through her veins reflected in Trent's gaze. He helped her settle into a chair and took the one across from her. Had it really only been two weeks since they sat in these exact same chairs?

Bella slid a wrapped package in front of Kat and a plate of food in front of Trent.

"Wow, are we already the predictable married couple?"

"We're not married yet," Kat launched back and ripped open the package. Inside was a hand-carved frame with the words *First Impressions* etched in the bottom. The picture was of Kat and Trent, the first day they'd sat at this table.

Kat blinked a couple of times to keep the tears from spilling. "How did you?"

Trent took the frame from her trembling fingers and laughed.

Bella shrugged. "I don't know why I snapped it. There was something about the way the air changed between you two that morning. It gave me goosebumps, and I took it while you were bickering."

Kat hopped up and hugged her dear friend. "Thank you."

Trent forked a pile of eggs into his mouth. And gestured to his plate. "And thank you."

Kat sat back down and stared at the frame. The picture captured that moment Kat had felt two weeks ago when she was more aware of them as a unit than as two separate people.

"Honey, you okay?"

She looked up and smiled. "I've never been better."

He nodded toward the frame. "Two weeks to love."

"And a lifetime to live," she answered, believing in her heart that together their life would be full of laughter and love and amazing moments of joy.

Epilogue

TRENT SLID THE COOKIE TRAY INTO THE FREEZER AND SHUT the door. He glanced around to the whiteboard where the list of tasks marched along in a row that he never thought he would accomplish.

"Kat?"

"Out here."

He wiped his hands on his apron and walked from the kitchen into the main part of the bakery. Kat was balancing on the side of a ladder, attempting to list the specials of the day.

He hurried over and steadied it. "Why didn't you ask me to get the board down for you?"

She finished a curlicue at the end of *Chai Pear Scones* and sighed. "There." She stepped down and kissed his cheek. "I didn't want to bother the maestro in his kitchen."

"It's our kitchen."

"No, no. I'm perfectly willing to concede all operations back there"—she waved her hand—"to you. I'm the word person. The marketing person."

"The amazing person."

Kat shrugged and Trent kissed her soundly. "Do you think we can do this?"

He hated that his uncertainty was broadcasted loud and clear in the tenor of his voice. Kat's gaze softened, and she cupped his cheek. "Dear, there's nothing the two of us can't do."

He grinned. "Speaking of the two of us, how's our personal bun in the oven doing?" He ran his hand over the tiny swell of Kat's belly.

"We're fine. A little hungry. Perhaps another sampling just to make sure everything is perfect for the opening tomorrow."

"I knew it. You married me for my baking skills."

She pulled him tight against her. "I married you for a whole host of skills you possess." She ran her hand down his back and squeezed his ass. "But for right now, sure let's go with your baking skills. Tonight, you can maybe see if some of your others can top that."

He followed her back into the kitchen where a batch of iced sugar cookies in the shapes of books and footballs sat, a nod to the bakery's name.

He poured two glasses of milk and settled in beside Kat on a stool.

"To us."

"To us." She clinked his glass. "And to the Books and Balls Bakery."

They took a sip and Kat bit into a cookie. "You know, if I wrote this into a book no one would believe it."

"Why, cause a writer not having great grammar is so uncommon?"

"Maybe I should start writing mysteries. I think I might know who my first victim will be."

"Honey, I was your victim the first time you jutted your chin out at me with no recognition."

Kat grew weepy and Trent closed in. "Please don't cry. I can't stand it. It rips me open."

"They're happy tears."

He snorted. "I'm not sure I believe there is such a thing as happy tears. Tears are tears."

"Just as love is love."

Trent pulled her close and kissed her forehead, thanking fate for bringing him this amazing woman to share a life with. A life richer and sweeter than anything he could have created alone.

Acknowledgments

Heath, for not batting an eye when I told you I was going to try something new. Thank you for your unwavering support.
Karen, for being a lifeline in this crazy sea of publishing.
Lee, your friendship all these years provides strength during the difficult times.
Laura, for connecting to my voice many years ago and for guiding this story to a beautiful end result. Thank you.
Holly, for working your cover copy magic and polishing my story to a shine.
Lyndsey, for creating a magical cover worthy of the love story inside.
My girls, I hope momma continues to make you as proud as you both make me every day.

About the Author

Contemporary romance author, Jennifer Hoopes, lives in a small town in Pennsylvania with her husband, and two daughters. Add two cats and a dog and sometimes the fur flies. Stories have been in her head for as long as she recognized every person had one and figuring out how two people meet and fall in love makes for a rewarding dream job.

When not writing she wears the many mom hats of PTO, dance, and music, all while driving a mean, mom-taxi. She loves caramel and roller coasters, plays a solo version of Carpool Karaoke, and cannot live without coffee and Jane Austen adaptations.